Perry Ripple Murder

A SPIES AND FOOD TRUCK COZY MYSTERY BOOK 4

ROSIE A. POINT

You're invited!

Hi there, reader!

I'd like to formally invite you to join my awesome community of readers. We love to chat about cozy mysteries, cooking, and pets.

It's super fun because I get to share chapters from yet-to-be-released books, fun recipes, pictures, and do giveaways with the people who enjoy my stories the most.

So whether you're a new reader or you've been enjoying my stories for a while, you can catch up with other like-minded readers, and get lots of cool content by visiting my website at *www.rosiepointbooks.com* and signing up for my mailing list.

Or simply search for me on *www.bookbub.com* and follow me there.

I look forward to getting to know you better.

Let's get into the story!

Yours,
Rosie

$O_{n\varepsilon}$

WINTER WAS MY FAVORITE TIME OF THE YEAR, but the last thing I'd expected on a crisp fall morning in October was to wake up to a blanket of white snow. Mostly because I was used to temperate winters, and Wisconsin was anything but temperate.

I drew back the thick cream drapes in my bedroom in the Cakeville Chateau, the ostentatiously named inn we'd chosen as our vacation spot for the colder months, and peered out at the eerily quiet snowscape.

"So much for ice cream," I said, and got out of bed.

It had been over a month since our rushed departure from Carmel Springs, and in that time, life had been blissfully quiet. We'd spent our days on the ice cream truck serving hot beverages and holiday flavors like Pumpkin Spice Delight and enjoying life.

I didn't want that to end, but it looked like a snow day if ever I'd seen one.

A knock rattled my thick wood bedroom door, just as I'd put the finishing touches on my make up.

"Coming!" I opened up to find Hentie waiting out in the hall, wearing a knit sweater covered in colorful circles and a bright smile. She held Sir Barkington the Blaf against her chest, the Chihuahua looking like a caramel-colored gentleman in a snazzy tartan waistcoat and matching booties.

"Did you see?" she asked. "Dit sneeu! It's snowing. I can't believe it. I've only seen snow a handful of times. Can we go outside and build a snowman?"

I chuckled at her childlike joy. It was nice that she was enthusiastic. The irony being that while I loved winter, I wasn't a fan of freezing my fingers off in the snow. "Let's wait until after we've had our morning coffee."

With that, we set off down the hallway together, past framed pictures of the inn's cat and her owner. The Cakeville Chateau was the epitome of eccentricity, and I loved that. The cream wainscoting was trimmed in baby pinks, and there were reading nooks with windows that looked out on the grounds.

The NSIB would never have approved our stay here without Smulder's prompting, and without Hentie offering to pay for half. Not that she realized a government organization was involved in how we selected which guest-houses and inns we stayed at.

Hentie and I entered the open plan dining area that led into the living room and took our seats in two cushy pink armchairs in front of the crackling grate.

There were a couple of guests already out of bed, chatting in clusters around the room, waiting for our hostess to make her appearance.

"What do you think she'll be wearing this morning?" Hentie asked, pinching and adjusting the messy gray bun atop her head. Barkington yapped and wagged his tail, insisting on being included in the conversation.

"A pink polka dot scarf wrapped around her head," I said.

"Huh." Hentie wriggled her nose from side-to-side. We played this game every morning. Guess what Edna Louise Pitt, our hostess, would arrive wearing for breakfast. Winner got the last cream puff on the plate.

"Time's a ticking, Hentie. She could arrive any minute."

"Ek weet nie. I don't know. Yesterday, she wore that velvet jacket. And the day before that was a feathered headdress."

"Uh huh."

"I think she's going to wear a pair of bright pink stilettos with rhinestones on them."

A bell chimed in the Cakeville Chateau, and the guests hushed at the sound of footsteps in the wooden hall.

"Good morning, my lovelies," Edna said, sweeping into the room, her arms thrown wide. Edna had freckles across her upturned nose, ever-pink cheeks and kind eyes. And she was wearing a pink polka dot scarf wrapped around her head.

"How do you keep doing this?" Hentie hissed.

"That's beside the point," I said. "You're three and zero, and that cream puff is mine."

"You're cheating, jong. I don't know how, but you're cheating."

I grinned broadly.

A few of the guests applauded Edna's *fabulous* arrival, and she bowed her head in their direction. "This morning's breakfast will be served shortly, dears. Please, sit down, enjoy your refreshments. As always the cream puffs are complimentary." And then she clapped her hands once.

The doors to the kitchen swung open, and the harried server, Niles, rushed out, wearing a suit and a bow tie—which was always skewed and splodged with food. He set up the coffee station on the breakfront sideboard then rushed back into the kitchen to get the cream puffs.

"Poor guy looks like he needs a vacation," Smulder

said, as he approached our comfy area and took the third armchair. "Who got the cream puff today?"

Hentie clicked her tongue, and I grinned.

"She's cheating. I know it," my friend said.

Smulder gave me a look that was fraught with meaning. The meaning being, stop being so good at snooping out what Edna was going to wear. He was my spy babysitter, and he was always afraid that I would give the game away.

Before I could get too irritated, Smulder grabbed a newspaper from the nearby table and started reading.

"Are we going out on the truck today?" Hentie asked.

"Not in this snow. We'll wait for them to plow the snow and then we can go exploring." Thankfully, our ice cream truck was equipped with defrosters. "If you want to go out in this weather."

"I want to build a snowman," Hentie said.

Smulder made a noise in his throat.

"What? I've never seen this much snow," Hentie said. "It's not like I'm dumb for wanting to have some fun." Barkington backed her up with a few choice barks directed toward Smulder.

"It's not that," he said. "I was reading the newspaper. This article is interesting." He folded the paper, *The Cakeville Chatter*, so that we could read it and plopped it down on the coffee table between us. "I'll grab us coffee." And then he got up and left us.

My stomach twirled. It was silly, but whenever Smulder did anything nice, it reminded me of a night in Carmel Springs when he'd leaned in, and I could have sworn he was about to kiss me.

Nope. I wasn't ready for that.

Instead of thinking about it, I lifted the newspaper and held it so that Hentie could read it as well.

The Unsolved Case of the Halloween Killer: Will the Murderer Strike Again This Year?

It's been five years since the last Halloween murder, and the Casey County Sheriff's Department is no closer to solving the crime. The killings, taking place on Halloween every few years, have gone unsolved for two decades with no new leads or persons of interest. When reached for comment, Sheriff Harry Stalz had this to say, "As always we're open to tips or hints from the public. This is still an ongoing investigation and, as such, I can't comment about it. We're encouraging citizens of Cakeville, Browning, and Piemonte, to be vigilant this Halloween, during the festivities, and to report any suspicious activity to your local sheriff's department or the Piemonte Police Station."

Sheriff Harry Stalz, recently elected after his heroic efforts to save two teenage girls from drowning in the Kerry Creek, has taken it upon himself to set up a task force to deal with the case. A refreshing change after the inaction from the previous sheriff who held the position.

"I forgot it was almost Halloween," I said. "Just a couple more days, right?"

"I wonder how they're going to decorate in the snow," Hentie said, then accepted a cup from Smulder.

"I'm sure everything will be fine this year." Smulder's words were almost forceful, as if he could will it to be that way.

The last thing we needed was a dead body to turn up while we were in town.

Two

A SNOW PLOW RATTLED BY IN THE STREET, PAST stone and brick houses with porches that had already been decorated for Halloween. The only building on Puff Street that hadn't been decked out with bats or creepy streamers, skeletons or carved pumpkins was the Cakeville Chateau.

Edna wasn't the type to celebrate the macabre or darker side of human nature. She was very much about pinks, creams, tasty foods and cute animals.

I stood at the top of the steps on the inn's porch, my arms folded and my breath misting in front of me as Hentie frolicked, mittens on, balling snow and laughing maniacally. The tip of her nose was pink, and her eyes were watery, but the cold didn't deter her.

I had to admire her spirit, even if I didn't necessarily get it. Snow in October wasn't for me. I didn't see how it could possibly fit with Halloween, or why we'd been banished to this state to endure the freezing temperatures.

Maybe, Special Agent in Charge Grant thought the snow would stop me from snooping, sleuthing, or causing any trouble.

Hentie lifted a snowball and lobbed it at me, I dodged it and laughed at her antics. "Glad to see you're having fun." Hentie had been reserved after we'd left Carmel Springs. "I heard from Sam yesterday," I called out. "The Oceanside is all prepped and ready for winter. Apparently, they're having a Halloween festival themselves."

Hentie's face fell. "Oh."

Darn. I'd put my foot in it. I'd wanted to cheer her up, but I'd upset her instead.

Hentie dropped the snowball in her hand and trudged through the snow toward the steps.

"Careful," I said, as she walked up them. I held out a hand.

She held it and we went back inside together, the warmth a welcome relief. Hentie stripped off her mittens, frowning at me, a full-length portrait of Edna and her cat, Kerfuffle, adding weight to her displeasure.

"What's up?" I asked.

"There's something funky going on with you, April," Hentie said.

"What do you mean?" I asked, raising an eyebrow.

Hentie would never know my real identity, nor would she be privy to the information that I wasn't a harmless ice cream truck entrepreneur. Rather I was a spy on the run.

"There's something that you're not telling me," Hentie said.

"Huh?"

"Come on, April, the truth will set you free."

"I honestly have no idea what you're talking about." It stung that I had to lie to her, but the alternative was her life being in danger. And Barkington's too. The dog pattered down the hall to join us, adorable in his tartan booties, and Hentie lifted him and hugged him.

"Listen, I've been around on this earth for sixty plus years now, and I can smell a load from ten kilometers away."

"Kilometers?"

Hentie sniffed. "Six miles give or take."

"I haven't lied to you about anything."

"Then why did you make us leave the Oceanside so quickly? Why did we abandon Sam when she needed us the most? She was in jail when we left. And both you and Oliver were acting weird. Julle is nie lekker nie, jy weet?" Oliver was Smulder's cover name.

"We left because it was time to move on," I said. "I didn't like the murders that were happening in Carmel Springs. It felt unsafe."

"Does that mean you want to leave now?"

"No?"

"But what about the Halloween murders in the newspaper?" Hentie asked. "If you're really that worried, why don't you want to leave now, huh?"

She had me there. "I'm like that, Hentie," I said.

"Like what?"

"I like to move around a lot. I don't like to stay put in one place. And I don't usually make friends or connections with people." Which was half true. When I made connections or friendships, I struggled to let them go or to do my job.

"So you wanted to leave just because?"

"I guess," I said.

"But you said it was the murders that bothered you," Hentie said. "So which is it?"

"Why can't it be both?" I asked. "Hentie, I think you're reading a little too much into this. Everything's fine." *And here I go with the gaslighting.* I hated this part of my job.

Hentie folded her arms in her puffy coat, frowning at me. "Okay, April. If you say so."

The guilt was almost too much to handle. A part of me wanted to break and tell her everything, but I couldn't do that without endangering her further and—

A door clicked, and Smulder came out onto the porch

stamping his boots on the wooden boards. "Nice morning, huh?"

"If by nice you mean cold enough to freeze your insides, then sure," I said.

He chuckled, and the tension dissolved.

"It's lekker, man," Hentie said. "I'm going to build my snowman now. Do you want to help me?"

"I think I'll pass," Smulder said. "I wanted to talk to April about the truck, actually."

"Oh, what about it?" I asked.

Hentie wandered off to start frolicking again.

Smulder waited until she was out of ear shot. "You good?"

"What?"

"Are you good?" he asked. "Because it looked like you were about to make a mistake. A big one."

"Oliver, I have no idea what you're talking about," I said, sweetly, then turned and started toward the thick wooden front doors.

Brian caught my arm. "Wait."

I glared down at the point of contact then looked up at him. "Since we're on the topic of big mistakes, would you look at what you're doing here?" I gestured to his hand.

He let go of me. "Were you or were you not going to tell Hentie our secret?" The words were murmured.

"I was not," I said. "Trust me, you have nothing to worry about."

"Stop it, April."

"Stop what?"

"Feeling guilty," he said. "Worrying that you're doing the wrong things by her. You have a duty to your country that comes first. You understand that, right?"

"Yes, but she's a part of our country now. She's married to—"

"That's not what I mean, and you know it," Smulder said. "Our duties come first, our friendships and relationships come second or not at all. This is the life we chose."

"And you're happy with that?" I asked. "It doesn't bother you that you'll never have real friends outside of our organization? You don't care that you can never get married? Have kids, pets? A family. A home that isn't always under threat?"

Brian lifted his chin. "I chose this," he said. "And so did you."

"Yeah," I whispered. "You're right." And then I brushed past him and entered the Cakeville Chateau. This time he didn't try to stop me. I didn't blame him for being worried. I *had* been close to letting something slip.

The Delta from a couple of months ago would never have done that. Or maybe she would have. Maybe the real

Delta was waiting for the chance to make real friends and attachments and—

I kicked off my boots and set them neatly beside a polished table in the foyer. These were thoughts for another time. Or for never.

As much as I hated to admit it, even to myself, Smulder was right.

Three

Two days later...

EDNA HAD DECIDED THAT WHILE HALLOWEEN decorations were "the most garish, offensive creations in existence", a Halloween pre-party was the perfect way to celebrate without being overtly grim. Which meant while the party was for Halloween, no costumes were allowed, and the decorations were frilly and pink, the music soothing. Which was kind of nightmarish in and of itself.

Our hostess had managed to make a creepy Halloween party without even trying, and the irony put a smile on my face as I stood near the fireplace in the Cakeville Chateau's open plan dining area, with a glass of champagne in hand, complete with a strawberry floating in the bottom.

How Edna had managed to find strawberries was a mystery I was happy to leave unsolved.

"This is interesting," Hentie said, and adjusted the black cape she'd chosen to pair with her velvet pantsuit this evening. She'd chosen the outfit to emulate the appearance of a vampire without actually wearing a costume. Skirting Edna's rules.

Barkington sat in an armchair beside the fire in a velvet waistcoat that matched Hentie's fit, and Smulder wasn't in attendance. Which was nice.

The more time I spent around him, the more my head hurt.

"It's not that bad," I said, and sipped my champagne. "At least there are cream puffs."

Servers in pink bow ties moved through the room holding silver platters of cream puffs and offering them to the attendees with exaggerated bows and smiles.

"So, what do you think?" I asked. "Want to mingle?"

"Ag, sure, why not?" Hentie lifted Barkington and tucked him under her arm. "There's got to be someone interesting to talk to around here." And off she went.

I took another sip of champagne before starting my rounds of the room. One of the small pleasures of being a spy undercover in small towns was that I got to meet people, to listen to their life stories. I'd always imagined I'd write a book about my life one day, but I doubted that would ever come to fruition. The NSIB wouldn't allow it.

Smulders' words came back to me, along with the picture perfect memory of him telling me that I had a duty to fulfill. The country came first.

Another layer of guilt to add onto a particularly foul cake that was laden with it.

"—knew you would come, Sheriff Stalz," Edna said, breathlessly. "I'm so honored that you'd grace us with your presence at my little soiree."

"Wouldn't miss it for the world, Edna." The sheriff stood beside our hostess. Tall with a round head that was too big for his body, he wore a look of patience as Edna took his arm and leaned against him. He was in his forties, from my estimation, whereas Edna's age was a purposeful mystery.

"But to have the hero of our town here. Gosh, it's such an honor."

"I'm not a hero," he said, and a couple of the other guests wandered over to listen in, almost like it was a play in action. "I was in the right place at the right time." Sheriff Stalz' cheeks pinked at the extra attention, and he scanned the room.

Stalz' gaze landed on me, and he smiled. "Hello," he said. "You must be new to our town."

"April Waters," I said, coming over. I'd opted for a modest red dress this evening, ruched at the top, with long sleeves. Red was my favorite color. "I run an ice cream truck with my friends."

"Ice cream?" Stalz asked. "In this weather?"

"Not so much," I agreed. "But we've sort of switched to serving hot beverages for the winter. Not that we can get out on the street much with the snow."

"It's clearing up now, though," Edna said, with a simpering laugh and a squeeze of the sheriff's arm. "And thank goodness for that. The children need to trick-or-treat."

"Do they?" That came from a woman in another group who'd been listening in on the conversation. She had two harsh black slashes for eyebrows and a sharp, pulled set to her face. Her dark eyes narrowed. "Come on, Edna, even you aren't that obtuse. Halloween is basically a kill zone in this town."

Sheriff Stalz cleared his throat. "Now, there's no need to panic about that. There's no evidence that whoever caused those killings is still operating in town. And you can rest assured that we will find the person responsible."

"Oh, I highly doubt that," the woman said. "This killer has been terrorizing Cakeville for years. What makes you think you can do any better than the last sheriff?"

The guests turned their heads as if watching a tennis match.

"That's enough, Juniper," Edna snapped. "We're trying to enjoy the party. There's no need to be cruel to the sheriff. He's a man of honor. If he says that he'll solve the crimes, then he'll solve the crimes."

"Yeah, well, I'll believe that when I see it." Juniper turned her back on them.

"So, ice cream," Stalz said, with an awkward chuckle. "How did you get into that business?"

Hentie had drifted over, Barkington in hand as he'd asked the question.

"It's always been a passion of mine," I said. "Ever since I tasted my first scoop of ice cream. Before I bought this truck, I owned a gelato truck as well."

"Interesting," he said. "And you what, travel the country serving ice cream? How does that work, financially?"

"My aunt left me money," I said. "So I can afford to follow my passions."

Hentie watched the exchange with a great deal of interest, and, oof, there was another layer of that guilt slathered on top of the last one. We talked about our lives on occasion, but Hentie hadn't cross-questioned me about how I'd come to be on board the truck in the first place. We took things day-by-day, and I preferred it that way.

The sheriff was about as nosy as I was, and he opened his mouth, no doubt to ask a follow-up question.

"If you'll excuse me," I said, and headed for the archway that led out of the dining area. In the hall, I took a breather and walked into the entertaining area that was hardly ever used—at least while we'd been at the inn.

The curtains were parted, showing off the snowy night, the Halloween decorations across the street, the houses with spooky skeletons and flashing lights and—

A shape moved between the buildings.

I stood still in the darkness, watching.

The shadowy figure crept into the street then hurried across it, heading for the Cakeville Chateau, passing beneath the circle of light from a lamppost. A man, with bushy eyebrows, a stern stare, and owlish eyes. He wore a black puffy jacket and gloves, and he didn't knock on the inn's front door.

Instead, he walked around the side of it.

What's that about?

Why would a random person be creeping around the inn at this time of the night? And when everyone was busy at the party.

Murderer.

The thought gave me a chill.

A shout rang out in the dining area, followed by the crash of breaking glass.

Four

I RUSHED INTO THE OTHER ROOM AGAIN, MY heels tapping on the wooden floor, half-expecting to find another dead body. But instead of a corpse, I found an altercation—two women stood across from each other, fists on their hips.

The first was the sharp-faced woman from earlier, Juniper, who'd made the untoward comment about the sheriff. And the second was younger, with a round face and kind blue eyes.

"You should be ashamed of yourself for coming here," Juniper said.

"I'm sorry, Juniper," the younger woman replied. "I didn't mean to bump into you."

A server, his pink bow-tie immaculate, hurriedly swept the remains of a champagne glass into a plastic dustpan under Edna's watchful eye. Sheriff Stalz stood nearby with a gaggle of admirers, both men and women, their focus on the ongoing argument.

Juniper, who wore a long black shawl draped over her shoulders, glared down her nose at the other woman. In the background, the fire crackled and popped.

Barkington, who had been quiet all evening, barked from Hentie's arms, and I walked over to join them. "They bumped into each other?" I asked.

"No, the younger one rammed into that Juniper woman," Hentie said. "I don't know if it was on purpose. I didn't see."

And the awkward quiet between the women thickened.

"Do you think I don't know what your intentions are?" Juniper asked. "Like I said, you should be ashamed to show your face here, Celeste."

"I—"

"After everything that you've done," Juniper said, raising her voice. "After the way you made a mockery of the citizens of Cakeville?"

"I didn't do anything wrong," Celeste said, stiffening. "And I'm here because I was invited. Isn't that right, Edna?"

The hostess looked up and gave a simpering non-response. She took several steps backward, away from

Juniper. "Now, let's not disturb this lovely Halloween party with icky details like that, dears. Come on, we have a lot to celebrate."

"Like what, Edna?" Juniper asked. "I've worked hard to make sure that this business is free of people like her, yet you invited her to your party." Juniper waggled a finger under Celeste's nose. "I thought I taught you a lesson, young lady."

"Wat op aarde gaan aan?" Hentie asked.

I took a snapshot of the women standing together and filed it away in my mind. Not that it mattered.

"You took everything from me," Celeste whispered.

Gasps and murmurs ran through the living room. When we'd first arrived in Cakeville, we hadn't anticipated that the town and its people would be this *dramatic*.

"I did what was good for this town," Juniper replied coldly. "What did you expect?"

"I expected support. I expected that the person I saw as a friend would treat me with care, would help me rather than get my bakery shut down." The words trembled as she said them.

"I don't feel sorry for you," Juniper replied. "You were giving people food poisoning."

"That's a lie," Celeste squeaked. "I didn't make anyone sick. I would never make anyone sick. You did this because you were jealous."

23

Juniper gave what could be classed as an unladylike snort. Not that I believed ladies had to behave in a prim and proper fashion. There was nothing like a good old fashioned punch to the throat to set a bad guy straight.

"Don't snort at me," Celeste snapped, gaining steam now that the audience was paying attention. One of the servers had even turned down the relaxing background music. "You wanted my bakery closed down because I was outselling you. You couldn't stand the competition."

"That's patently ridiculous," Juniper replied. "I didn't have to get your bakery shut down. That was the health inspector's prerogative." And then she waved a hand. "It's obscene that you decided to come to this party when the people here know what type of person you are. The kind who poisons people and who—"

"I am not going to stand here and listen to this," Celeste said, and then she spun on her heel and walked for the archway that led to the foyer.

"Good riddance," Juniper said, tossing her dark hair. She sort of reminded me of Morticia Adams. "Can you believe the nerve of that woman?"

Sheriff Stalz adjusted his belt. "Juniper, you didn't have to be—"

"Get real, Stalz," the baker said. "You of all people know how important it is to protect the people of this town."

"Don't compare yourself to Sheriff Stalz," Edna said. "He's a true hero." And then Edna clapped her hands and had the servers turn up the music again and start circulating the room with their platters, putting an end to the argument.

Juniper engaged in conversation with another woman who looked like she rued the day she'd been born.

"I guess this is not going to be as quiet of a vacation as we thought," I said.

Hentie chuckled and stroked Barkington's ears.

"Excuse me," I said. "Ladies' room." And then I exited the room, my mind on the man I had seen creeping down the side of the inn. I walked down the long hall, flanked by doors that led into suites, until I reached the enclosed and heated back porch.

But I wasn't alone.

Celeste stood staring out of the window at the snowy backyard. Which was empty. No stranger in sight.

"Sorry," I said. "I didn't think anyone would be back here."

"It's fine," Celeste said, gesturing that I should stay. "I came back here for a breather. I was going to leave, but I thought, you know what? Why should I let that rude, evil wretch chase me off. Nobody actually believes what she says."

"That was intense," I said. "The argument."

"Yeah, everything with Juniper is intense. She likes to fight and she likes to bring other people down with her, no matter what the scenario." Celeste shook her head. "I—I never thought I'd say it, but I hate that woman. I hate her with a fiery passion."

"I'm sorry," I said smoothly. "For what it's worth, I doubt anyone believed her."

"Oh no, they wouldn't. Everyone in Cakeville knows what kind of person she is," Celeste said. "She called the health inspector on my bakery, and she planted things in my refrigerator to get me shut down. Juniper is ruthless. She'll do anything to advance her own goals, and that includes embarrassing me." Then she sighed and pressed a hand to her face. "Sorry, I'm ranting."

"That's all right. I can imagine you're frustrated."

"Frustrated? I'd love to throttle her and teach her a lesson," Celeste said. "But of course, that wouldn't change anything. Besides, I'm done with cookies and cupcakes. I'd much rather spend my time on something worthwhile. Like books." And then she fell quiet and hugged herself, staring out at the winter landscape.

"It was nice to meet you."

"You too." Celeste raised an eyebrow at me.

"April," I said, pressing a hand to my chest. "April Waters."

"Celeste Chills," she replied. "Of Chills Bookstore.

You should come by in the week. We've got a book for every taste."

"Thank you, I will." And then I left her on the porch and headed back up the hall. The strange man was gone, and the party was in full swing again, people eating, laughing and chattering about the evening's events.

My gut said that this wasn't the last weird encounter we'd have in the Cakeville Chateau.

Five

I LET HENTIE WIN THE CREAM PUFF BET THE NEXT morning, because I was starting to gain weight, but partly because she was already starting to get suspicious that I was cheating. Was it cheating to be a spy and have a sense of what a person would wear? Or that I had a skeleton key that had effectively given me access to Edna's private room and her closet which was stacked with her outfits, arranged by the day on which she'd wear them?

Okay, that last part was definitely cheating, but there were cream puffs to be won here. What was I supposed to do? Play fair?

The minute that delicious creamy, sweet puff had touched my lips on the first day we'd eaten at the Cakeville Chateau, I'd been a goner.

I sipped my coffee while Hentie ate her last cream puff.

Today, we'd taken a table rather than the set of armchairs in front of the fire. Barkington lapped up water from a bowl covered in blue pawprints beside our table.

"Ooh, that's lekker," Hentie said, after she'd finished her treat. "I'm going to be the size of a house before we leave."

"Me too," I said.

Hentie narrowed her eyes. "You didn't let me win, did you?"

"Of course not," I said. "It's a guessing game. You guessed correctly. Who could have predicted that Edna would decide to wear a full feather headdress to breakfast this morning?"

"She must be in a fancy mood after the Halloween party."

I wriggled my nose and watched our host operate from across the room. She would sweep from table to table, clasping her hands together and bowing her head to ask the guests how they were enjoying their stay. But the bowed head led to the feathers in her headdress, pink and white and long, brushing over people's faces. A couple of the guests had either sneezed or batted the feathers out of the way, nearly knocking Edna backward.

Breakfast with a show. *They should put that on their Booking.com listing.*

"What are the plans for today?" I asked Hentie. "Do

29

you want to try to set up the truck and sell some hot chocolate? Or would you prefer to take it easy?"

"It's Halloween," Hentie said. "I'd love to go out and see the displays around town. How much fun would that be?" Her tone was hopeful. Hentie hadn't celebrated many Halloweens. Apparently, they weren't as much of a thing in South Africa.

"Okay, that sounds good to me."

Smulder entered the dining room, fresh, cleanly shaven, wearing a long-sleeved white shirt and a pair of blue jeans. He could have stepped off the cover of a magazine, but I refused to be affected. I just had to wait for the butterflies in my stomach to get the message.

Smulder gave me an easy smile, and my stomach did a manic dance. I lifted a hand in return, keeping it casual, keeping it cool.

"If you stare any harder, your eyes are going to pop out of your head, April," Hentie remarked, just as I'd taken a sip of coffee.

I choked and sprayed coffee down my front.

Brian, who'd been three steps from the table, slowed, grimacing.

Hentie burst out laughing and held out her cloth napkin, which I took, less than gratefully, and used to clean myself.

By the time I looked up, Smulder was embroiled in a

conversation with Edna, who was shorter than him, and kept turning her head as she talked, tickling the underside of Smulder's nose. It would have been funny, if I hadn't thoroughly humiliated myself two seconds earlier.

"So," I said, after another sip of coffee. "You want to go out and see the decor. We can do that. I'm sure there are even better displays further down the street or in town."

"Yay!" Hentie clapped her hands. "Ek kan nie wag nie! I can't wait."

"I appreciate you translating your Afrikaans."

"Yes, well it's my plan to get you to speak it," she said, tapping the side of her nose.

We finished off our breakfast—maple pancakes, cream puffs, and bacon—then took Barkington to Hentie's room. He was set up with food, water and a pee pad in case he needed the bathroom.

"Don't worry, Bark," I said, "it's a quick excursion. We'll be back in no time. Are you sure you don't want to bring him with us?"

Hentie gave Barkington a kiss on the nose. "He's not made for cold weather. I want us to be able to get out and explore a bit. If we were just going out on the truck and he could stay in his crate with his warm blanket and the heating, then maybe, but not this time."

We said our farewells to Barkington, who had already grabbed his favorite chew toy and was laying into it, and locked the bedroom door. We put on our coats and our boots, our scarves and gloves, and headed out.

The road had been cleared of snow, and the front path that led down to it had been de-iced. Still, Hentie and I clasped hands as we walked toward the gate that led onto the street. Our truck was parked in a space in front of the inn, flanked by the other guests' cars, with a fresh layer of snow on top.

We were two steps into our journey when a horrified scream cut through the crisp morning air.

Hentie and I nearly tripped over each other in our haste to find the cause of the scream.

It came a second time.

"Help! Oh my gosh, help! Not again. This can't be happening again! Not my house!" The shouts had come from across the street.

Hentie and I checked both ways then crossed and found a woman standing in front of a brick two story home directly across from the Cakeville Chateau. She covered her face and peeked between her fingers. "No. It can't be."

"Hey," Hentie said. "What's going on? Why are you screaming?"

The woman gave a muted half-scream and dropped her hands, meeting Hentie's gaze and then mine. "It's happening again."

"What is?"

"The Halloween Killer is back." She pointed toward the display in front of the house.

Hentie and I turned our heads.

On the front lawn, the homeowner had set up a cauldron and a circle of witches in funny positions. The fake witches, made of plastic, were either bent over the cauldron or crouched beside it, and one of them was seated on a deck chair, as if they were on a beach. Except that witch wasn't plastic.

No, that witch was a corpse, positioned to hold a cup with a mini-umbrella poking over the rim. The hand that grasped the cup was pale cream turning blue. And the killer had placed a witches hat on her dark hair.

"Juniper," Hentie said. "April, dis Juniper."

I clasped my friend's hand to calm her down. "I'll call 911."

Six

I WAS PRONE TO TAKING SNAPSHOTS OF CRIME scenes. It was the easiest way for me to file away information, since I had an eidetic memory and could refer to it at any time. And while I didn't technically forget anything from the past, it was nice to bury unpleasant memories from my childhood. Even if I was, theoretically, burying them in images of corpses and suspects and clues.

Grim.

The scene was horrifying. The killer had to have strangled his victim, because there was no blood on the snow. But there was a shoe print.

A large one. Mens size 13 was my estimation. The mouth of the witch corpse was open, as if the jaw had dropped after death. The fingernails, well, they were bloodied as if she'd put up a fight.

But how had this happened?

We'd been right across the street. And the victim, Juniper, had been at the party with us.

And she had a confrontation with Celeste. Who had said she'd love to throttle Juniper. This didn't look good for her, but a threat wasn't proof.

Shortly after the 911 call, Sheriff Stalz arrived in his cruiser, the logo of the Casey County Sheriff's Department printed along its side. Stalz got out of the car wearing a frown. Several of his deputies pulled up shortly after and started separating people from the scene.

The owner of the house was drawn off to one side.

A few moments later, Edna came tottering across the street, wearing a luxurious faux fur coat. "Sheriff Stalz," she cried. "What's going—?" She spotted Juniper's body and gave a shrill screech.

"Edna," Stalz said, "would you be a dear and give my deputies access to your dining area? We'd like to question a few witnesses and doing that in the cold isn't—"

"It's the Halloween Killer, isn't it?" Edna asked. "They've struck again."

"It appears so," Stalz said, and his tone deepened with disapproval. "But we'll catch him. Whoever he is, we'll catch him. What do you say, Edna? Can we use your inn?"

"Of course, Sheriff Stalz. Anything to help."

A few deputies remained behind to deal with the scene

while Stalz herded us toward the guesthouse. Inside, we removed our outerwear then entered the dining area. A couple of the guests were still enjoying the last of their breakfasts. Smulder was seated in an armchair beside the fire, sipping coffee and reading a book.

The minute Stalz entered, Brian tensed. His gaze flickered toward me, and my insides sank. Oh boy, this wasn't going to go down well with my spy babysitter.

"April?" He got out of his chair. "What's going on?"

"I'm afraid you have to leave," Stalz said, to the room at large. "There's been an unfortunate incident, and the sheriff's department is going to use this dining room during our investigation of a crime."

Smulder's jaw tightened, a muscle hopping below his eye. Poor guy couldn't catch a break. It didn't matter where we went, danger followed. That or we'd just chosen the wrong town at the wrong time of year.

The guests gossiped as they filtered out of the room, some of them brazenly asking the sheriff for more details, but Stalz didn't answer, merely directed them out with a smile and assurances that the situation was under control.

Smulder was the last to leave, and he lingered under the archway, staring at me as if that would stop me from doing anything rash. As if *I* was the one causing the problem, not the Halloween Killer.

Already, the corkboard, cleared off after our last investigation, had taken its place in my mind. The image of the corpse was pinned to it. A thin red thread connected that image to another of the mens size 13 shoe print in the snow. A single print. Could it have been placed there to throw Stalz off the scent?

Smulder's feet were large, so were Stalz. Heck, the size of the shoe itself wasn't going to help me. There were plenty of men in Cakeville with large feet.

Three more images populated the board.

The stranger in that thick black coat who had sneaked around the inn.

Juniper and Celeste arguing in the dining area.

And a blurry picture that wouldn't show itself to me.

Not this again. Every time, my brain played tricks, as if testing whether I could put the puzzle pieces together on my own. What was the use in having an eidetic memory if my own gray matter wouldn't play ball?

Once the dining room was cleared out, Stalz guided me toward the armchairs in front of the fire and sat me down.

Hentie was taken off to the opposite side of the vast room with a deputy. And the homeowner stood near the front of the room with another surly law enforcement official, peering out of the window at the commotion outside.

"April, right?" Stalz asked, removing a pen and pad

from his pocket. "I'm sorry we're meeting again under such unfortunate circumstances."

"Yeah," I said. "It's April Waters."

Stalz nodded and took a note on his pad. "Talk to me about what you saw this morning."

I told him about our decision to go out and see the Halloween decorations, and hearing the scream from across the street.

"And you were the one who called 911?"

"Yes," I said. "I think she was too shaken up." I gestured toward the homeowner.

"Ursula," Stalz said. "She's lived across the street from the Cakeville Chateau for years. You're new, right? A guest at the inn?"

"Yeah." Obviously he had to ask for his investigation.

"Now, April," Stalz said, his tone serious. "Did you hear anything last night or in the early hours of this morning? Apart from the scream?"

"No," I said. "Nothing. But I did see a man sneaking around the inn last night during the Halloween party." I gave him the details, and he took copious notes.

"And how tall was he?"

"Average height," I said. "Probably around 5'10" or 5'11"?"

"All right. Thank you, April. You've been very helpful." He reached into his pocket and withdrew a card.

"This is the number for my office. If you think of anything that might help us catch who did this, please call me. Anything at all." He rose.

"I will," I said. "I suppose you think this has to be the Halloween Killer, right?"

"I can't say for sure yet. We need to examine the evidence," Stalz replied. "But it does fit his M.O."

"How so?"

"The killer always leaves a calling card," Stalz said. "A single shoe print on the scene. Anyway, I have to get to work. Call me if you think of anything else."

"Thank you, Sheriff Stalz. I will."

And then he headed for the door. He stopped to talk to one of the deputies before exiting the room.

The Halloween Killer was back. And I was intrigued. Not only were there other cases to consider, mysteries that might contain hidden clues, but we weren't under suspicion for once.

When Hentie was done with the deputy, she came over to me and took a seat in the armchair. The fire had burned low, so I carefully added more logs.

"What do you think?" Hentie asked.

"I think," I said, "that we should do an internet search once the cops are gone."

Hentie broke into a broad smile.

Seven

HENTIE BROUGHT HER PHONE OUT OF THE pocket of her pants suit—a teal color today to match the winter weather—and unlocked it. She typed furiously, the *tap-tap* of the keys building the anticipation.

I scooched my armchair closer so we could put our heads together.

Articles populated the search screen, all of them discussing the Halloween Killer with headlines that would have chilled a hardened detective. Or a spy who'd already seen too much.

Halloween Killer Strikes Again: Corpse Found Posed as Zombie Santa Claus

Another Halloween Killing? When Will the Reign of Terror End?

Why Haven't Local Law Enforcement Caught The Halloween Killer?

That last article was from years ago. Edna had mentioned that Sheriff Stalz would surely catch the killer now that he'd been elected, but I wasn't so sure. What could possibly have kept the cops from discovering the truth? What were they missing? And why—?

"April." Smulder placed a hand on my shoulder.

I pretended to get a fright, for Hentie's benefit. I'd heard the footsteps, though I hadn't cared to check who'd been approaching us.

"Oliver," Hentie said. "Listen, you will never believe it. There's another murder. That Halloween Killer has gone and done it again."

"That's terrible. Do you mind if I talk to you for a moment, April? Alone?"

"Sure," I said. "Be right back, Hentie."

"Will you grab Barkington from my room, asseblief?" Hentie asked, handing me her room key.

"Absolutely." I took the key from her, and Smulder followed me out into the hallway.

We walked in silence.

"Spit it out, will you?" I said. "There's no point dragging it out." I unlocked Hentie's bedroom door, and Barkington barked a greeting and pitter-pattered toward me. I picked him up and kissed his head, and he gave me a few cheek licks.

"You know what I'm going to say," he replied.

"That I shouldn't get involved in what doesn't concern me. That you'll be forced to tell Grandpa if I do." Grandpa was Special Agent in Charge Grant, who was probably a few calls away from a high blood pressure diagnosis.

"Look," Smulder said. "I'm not going to drag this out. Just don't do anything I wouldn't do."

"I'll be the most boring woman you've ever met until the case is solved."

"Wait, are you saying I'm boring?"

My insides squirmed. "No. That's not what I was saying. I misspoke."

"Huh." Brian took a step toward me. "You *really* think I'm boring?"

"I think you play by the rules," I said. "Nothing wrong with that."

"Some rules were made to be broken." He took another step toward me, so close that I lost my breath, and my mind shifted back to the night when he'd almost kissed me. Almost.

There was a breathless moment where Smulder lips parted, where it seemed like he would lean in and break the strange tension between us.

"But not these rules," he said, and took a step back,

clearing his throat. "Not the ones that were put in place by our superiors for your safety."

Barkington, who had watched the entire exchange, whined and barked at Smulder. I could always trust Bark to be on my side.

I gestured toward the door, and we exited Hentie's room. I locked it up tight and returned to the dining area alone. I didn't want to think about Smulder any more, or the strange games he was playing with my emotions, or even that he had the ability to toy with me.

"Blaffies," Hentie cried, as I deposited her handsome Chihuahua in her lap.

Barkington gave her several yips in greeting then settled in for cuddles and pets.

I gave Hentie a tight smile. "Where were we?"

Hentie wriggled her nose from side-to-side. "You were going to tell me what's really going on here."

"Huh?"

"Just now," she said, "you and Oliver left the room. Are you two dating?"

"Absolutely not."

"That's what I thought," Hentie said. "Then why don't you tell me the truth, April. I know something funky is going on here. You keep acting weird, and you're very good at solving mysteries."

"Hentie, I—"

"Wag net 'n bietjie. Wait a bit," she said. "Let me finish. You keep going off with Oliver and having private talks. And when you come back from them, you always look furious, like he's insulted your entire lineage. So what is going on? Who is he really? And who are you?"

It was such a straightforward question that my mouth went dry.

"Well? Come on, now. I've been around on this earth long enough to smell a load of horse poop when it's wafted in front of my nose. And you telling me everything is normal, and that we left Carmel Springs in such a rush was just for fun is a load of horse poop."

I opened my mouth, but Hentie waved a hand.

"Don't tell me you're afraid of murders," Hentie said, "because you and I both know that's not true."

Barkington gave me a stern look that matched Hentie's.

"Hentie," I said, and then I lost my words.

What was I supposed to say to her? That the person she knew was a lie? But that wasn't true either. I hadn't lied about the type of person I was, only my name and my real occupation.

"Whatever it is," Hentie said, "I want to know what you can tell me. I won't be offended that you didn't tell me the truth. Unless you're the one who's killing everybody."

I snorted a laugh. "Hentie, please."

But I couldn't follow it up with a platitude. She was staring at me with such sincerity, and she had become a close friend. I had struggled for a long time to trust people, and when I had finally let someone in—my boyfriend, Mickey, who had passed away—it was like the dam had broken.

I craved human companionship, though I had built my life around being alone. On being efficient. And it was difficult to reconcile those two parts of myself.

Barkington and Hentie watched me.

I lowered my voice. "There are things I can't tell you," I said. "If I do, it would put you in danger. It would put me in danger as well."

"Okay," Hentie said. "Then what can you tell me?"

I glanced around the room, but Smulder was nowhere to be seen. If he caught me talking to Hentie like this, he would ship me off before the words had gotten out of my mouth. Grant would have a conniption. The NSIB would punish me.

Duty first. Country first.

"That I'm on the run," I murmured. "That my identity is secret. That we may move from town to town frequently. And that I can't afford to have the truck or my name in the papers."

Hentie's eyes had gone wide. Barkington whined and lay down, covering his nose with a caramel-colored paw.

"Wow," Hentie said. "Goeie genade."

"Yeah. I'm trusting you with that information," I said.

"You hardly told me anything," Hentie said. "But it's enough. I will keep your secret, and I won't ask you any more questions."

She hadn't even asked who I was running from. If it was dangerous for her or for Bark.

"If you want to leave, you can," I said.

I could make sure the NSIB protected her too, if absolutely necessary. It would probably lead to me disappearing and going underground, but I was willing to do it to protect her.

"Ag, asseblief. I'm from South Africa. You think a few secrets and murders can scare me?" She laughed. "I'm staying."

I'd never felt such an overwhelming sense of relief.

I wanted to tell her as much, but before I could, Juniper walked into the dining room. Juniper, who should have been dead, whose corpse I had literally seen this morning, stopped beside our coffee table.

"Hello," she said, "with a pleasant smile. Is Edna around?"

Hentie turned and screamed in her face.

Eight

JUNIPER YELLED RIGHT BACK, JUMPING BACK A few feet and putting her hands up. Her fingers were no longer bloodied as if she'd fought off an attacker, but that was the least of our problems. The woman was alive. And kicking. And Sheriff Stalz was still out there processing her murder scene.

"What is wrong with you?" Juniper asked, glaring at Hentie, those dark slashes for eyebrows drawn down over brown eyes. "Are you trying to give me a heart attack?"

"Ek kan nie," Hentie said, babbling the words. "Ek kan nie! I can't. Dis te veel. Too much."

"What is this?" I asked, my heart rate had spiked at her presence, but I practiced my breathing to keep it under control.

"This is an inn," Juniper said. "Do you need medical attention? Does she?"

"No, but you should," I replied. "Was that your idea of a sick prank?"

"Was *what* my idea of a prank?" she asked.

Hentie sputtered, and I couldn't get the words out myself. I'd been around, I'd seen plenty, but a person faking their death in such a violent manner, then simply "coming back to life" and acting like nothing was wrong?

"Penelope!" Edna appeared in the doorway. She had changed her pink and white feathered headdress to an ostentatious black hat with a feather poking out of it. "Oh my dear, I just heard the news."

Juniper turned toward Edna. "What news?"

And then it clicked.

Hentie and I realized it at the same time, both of us turning toward each other, mouths dropping open.

This wasn't the deceased. This had to be her twin sister.

And now that I looked closely, with the shock of seeing a corpse reanimated gone, there were little differences. A dark spot over one eyebrow, a different twist to her mouth, but she was so similar to Juniper, it was breathtaking.

"You surely must have seen Sheriff Stalz outside," Edna said. "The police cars? The—The body."

"Oh," Penelope said, then turned to us. "Oh! Is that why you were screaming? I thought that was odd. Yeah, I saw her. Juniper finally got what was coming to her. She would have loved this, you know."

"What, my dear?" Edna sounded taken aback.

"The attention that her death is going to bring. To be the victim of the Halloween Killer is 'an honor' in her eyes. She told me that countless times. How these no good people who had died at the killer's hands didn't deserve the media attention." Penelope rolled her eyes theatrically. "Juniper was an attention hog."

"Oh, yes, she was a little difficult to be friends with but—"

"A *little difficult?*" Penelope laughed, touching her hand to her stomach. "I was her sister. I spent the majority of my childhood dealing with her tantrums and our parents' attempts to console her. She was an impossible human being."

So, no love lost between the sisters.

I took a mental image of her standing in front of Edna. The scowl on her face, her folded arms. "Of course, she had to die in a way that would draw attention."

"We're sorry for your loss," I said.

"Don't be," Penelope said. "We were basically estranged. The only time I heard from my sister was when she wanted something from me. Or when she was in the mood to gossip or had deigned to grace me with her presence. We were the opposite of what you'd expect of twins. No emotional connection." Penelope brushed strands of hair back from her face. "Anyway, I didn't mean to go on a rant, for heaven's sakes. I actually came to ask after you, Edna. I heard your party was a success."

Hentie's eyes were comically wide. Barkington tilted his head this way and that, listening to the humans talk.

I kept my expression neutral.

Edna and Penelope didn't wander off, but remained beside our spot.

"It was a success," Edna said, wearily. "But I doubt people will think of it that way. They're going to cancel Halloween."

"Cancel Halloween?" Penelope asked. "Unacceptable. This is the time of year where I sell the most curios."

"I'm sorry," Edna said. "Sheriff Stalz is taking this case seriously. He's determined to catch the killer."

"But what about the festival this weekend? The costume competition? The house decorating competition? We're famed for our Halloween!" Penelope folded her arms. "I won't allow this. We can't let Halloween go. For heaven's sake, this is what makes the town the most money thanks to tourism, and now it's being called off?"

"Sheriff Stalz—"

"I'll handle Stalz, Edna." Penelope's lips thinned. "Just

be ready to have your servers help me at my stall at the festival this weekend."

"All right, Penelope, but—"

"No buts. I won't let a silly killer stand in my way," Penelope said, and patted her chest. "Mama's gotta eat." And then she walked off. The front door tapped shut a moment later.

Edna stood there, staring into space, shell-shocked. "I —Well, goodness me."

"Are you okay?" Hentie asked her.

"I'm fine," she said. "Sorry you had to see that, dears. Would you like something to drink? I can summon Niles and request a round of cream puffs if that would help."

"We're good," I said. "Thanks, Edna."

"Good. Good." And then she walked off toward the kitchen. Halfway there, she shook her head, turned around and went to the foyer instead.

"Listen," Hentie said, after she was gone. "I've seen some crazy stuff in my time, but that took the cake. I really thought she came back to life."

"Me too," I said. "But it's even more disturbing that she's not bothered about her sister's death."

"Ja. She seems almost happy about it. I heard that people handle grief in different ways. Maybe that Halloween thing is how she's going to deal with her sister's passing."

I shrugged.

I didn't buy it.

Penelope had made our suspect list. Already, the image of her standing there, confronting Edna, had attached itself to my corkboard, a thin line spreading from it to the central image of the body.

But the print in the snow had been a man's shoe. And who would have the strength to carry a body and position it like that?

Unless the shoe was worn by a woman as a way to throw others off the trail. We needed to do more research, away from prying eyes. Particularly Brian's prying eyes.

"Meet me on the back porch in five minutes," I said. "I'm going to get my laptop."

Hentie gave me a grin and a thumbs up. Barkington barked a quick goodbye.

Thankfully, the hall was clear of Smulder or Edna. I glanced toward the closed doors, my heart racing after what we'd seen, and after the conversation I'd had with Hentie. My friend trusted me, even though she knew I'd lied to her and would continue to do so. Did that mean I could trust her too?

Nine

The Halloween Killer: A Deep Dive on the Terror Haunting Cakeville's Infamous Holiday Celebration

For two decades, Cakeville has been the target of a killer, the likes of which have never been seen before. The mysterious yet horrifying Halloween Killer who strikes only on the eve of Halloween, when the decorations have been put up and the town is ready for the upcoming festival.

Like something out of a horror movie, the killer has chosen several Halloween's to make their kills. The first victim, Belinda O' Toole, who was killed in 2004, was a grocery store clerk last seen at a party on the night before Halloween. She was found in her neighbor's front yard, dressed up as a vampire. Local police were stumped. There were no clues. And the last person who had seen Belinda, her boyfriend, was taken in for questioning, only to be released later due to a lack of evidence.

The second victim, killed during the Halloween celebrations of 2007, was none other than Gerald Stone, the crotchety local librarian who was known to throw stones at children who made a noise outside of the Cakeville Public Library. He was last seen on the morning of Halloween. He was found propped up on the library steps, dressed as a ghoul.

"This is grim stuff," I said, as I read through the article. I didn't have to take notes. I simply took an image of the article as I read through it, adding the slips of information to the corkboard.

Hentie shivered and nodded, as she sat back on a comfy chair on the enclosed porch. The snow had started falling again, though it was by no means thick, and we'd occasionally pause our research to chat, grab some coffee, have a snack or to stare at the back of the inn.

The backyard stretched out, rolling toward a line of snow covered trees and the start of the mountain that towered over the town. When we'd first arrived in

Cakeville, I'd stared up at the peak, picturing what the view would be like from the top.

The town wasn't just picturesque, it was perfect, with streets that intertwined and reminded me of a rabbit warren and the homes huddled together.

"Find anything yet?" Hentie asked, as she tapped on her screen.

"Only information about the killings, but there's more research to be done."

After the second death, the killer seemed to retreat for a while, and Cakeville fell into a false sense of calm and security. But that time of peace didn't last long. In 2014, an entire seven years after the last murder, two victims were claimed. Bennie and Robert McCall were found wearing Jack-o'-lanterns for heads. And when the police removed the carved pumpkins, they made a grisly discovery. Their heads were missing and were never found.

I grimaced. That meant the murders hadn't taken place at the crime scene. Otherwise there would have been a significant amount of blood.

But taking down two men? Surely, that had to be the work of another man. Unless the killer was drugging their victims and then murdering them? But to drag two bodies away from a crime scene, presumably load them into a car, and drive them over to be positioned at another location would take strength.

And then there were the time gaps to consider. The murders spanned two decades. Which meant the murderer had to be of a certain age. And what exactly was their modus operandi? Why would they always choose Halloween? Why display the corpses of their victims?

Unless it's to humiliate them.

There were two options that I could see.

Either, the killer wanted the attention. They wanted to be feared and respected.

Or they wanted to humiliate the victims and make a show of them.

It could be a combination of the two.

A picture of the alleged killer was building in my mind. A man, average height, large feet, big enough to overpower his victims.

Or, a woman, likely in her forties, strong, not slight, who knew how to use poisons or sedatives to get what she wanted. Perhaps, she'd had help?

Each time, the victims had been displayed in such public places, it begged the question, why not put up cameras if this was a recurring problem?

The crunch of boots in the snow brought me back to the present, and I looked up as a man dressed in a puffy black jacket and hiking boots rounded the side of the

Cakeville Chateau. He whistled under his breath, releasing a cloud of vapor.

"That's the guy," I said, and got up. "That's him. Hey! Hey, you!" I set my laptop on a side table and jumped up. I rushed to the porch door and unlocked it. I was greeted by a blast of chill air.

"Dis yslik koud," Hentie cried. "Close it. It's freezing!"

"You," I said. "Excuse me, sir."

The guy in the black coat turned and trudged over to me. He shouldered a heavy hiking backpack as he walked. "Yeah?" His beard was thick and wiry, specked with bits of snow. "What's up?"

"Who are you and what are you doing on the Cakeville's property?" I asked.

"Eh?"

"I saw you hanging around here last night," I said.

I wasn't usually this straightforward, but it was freezing, and I'd come up with a mental profile, albeit a blurry one, of the potential killer. This guy matched it. Average height, large shoes, and he'd been at the inn last night.

"Yeah, I was scouting out my hike for this morning," he said. "I've got permission from Edna." He grinned at me, showing two missing front teeth. "Wrenly Holmes." He bit the end of his glove and pulled it off then stuck out his hand. "Nice to make your acquaintance."

"April Waters." I shook his hand.

"Why are you yelling at me?" he asked. "There's been enough yelling going around."

"What do you mean?"

"Angry people. Always angry. I think it's the cold that makes 'em irritable. Don't blame 'em."

"You were here last night," I said. "Scouting?"

"Yeah. I like to get the lay of the land before I go on a hike. Look, I've been hiking this mountain for a while, and it's a fickle beast. People go missing in there, so, best to know what you're doing. Edna's kind enough to let me do survival trials and practice runs out here. Good ol' gal."

I absorbed the information.

"Only thing that's more fun than hiking is spelunking," he said, then waved a hand. "Gettin' ahead of myself. Why are you worried about where I am or what I'm doing? Did I give you a scare last night?"

"Yeah," I said, smiling. "You did. I didn't expect to see some guy in all black gear marching around the inn."

"Marching," he laughed. "Oh no, just prospecting."

"We're all a bit jumpy," Hentie put in, from her seat. "A woman was killed."

"Oh, I heard about that," Wrenly said. "It was, that, uh, what's her name? The one who kept getting businesses shut down."

"Juniper."

"That's her," he said, and his tone shifted in a way I didn't like.

"When last did you see her?"

"Who's asking? You a cop?"

"No. Just a nosy busybody," I said.

He chuckled. "Fair enough. I saw her last night on my way out of the woods." He pointed back to the treeline. "Saw her getting into a black car."

"Do you remember what time?"

Wrenly scratched his beard. "Oh, must've been around eleven at night, on account of the fact that I got home at half past, and it takes me about that long to get back home from the Chateau." He hesitated. "Look, I'd love to stay all day and talk to you lovely ladies, but I don't want to lose any more light than I already have. Nice to meet you."

"You too."

He trudged off, and I shut the porch door, staring at his retreating back. I took a snapshot of him and added it to the corkboard.

Ten

THE NEXT MORNING, AFTER WHAT FELT LIKE TWO hours of sleep, Hentie and I grabbed our coffee and cream puffs, too tired to wager over what Edna would wear this morning.

"You two are quiet," Smulder said, as he paged through the Cakeville Chatter. He narrowed his eyes. "What did you stay up all night doing?"

"Never question a lady about her private time," Hentie snapped at him. Barkington agreed vehemently.

Smulder raised his hands. "Just looking out for my two friends."

"I'm your boss," I said. "And Hentie's your colleague." It was harsh, but I was over-tired from spending last night researching the cases, and Smulder was a constant source of irritation. Every veiled look was a reminder or a judgment, and while he was just doing his job, it got under my skin.

Hentie patted Smulder on the arm. "Don't worry, Oliver, she'll be fine once she's finished her cream puffs."

"What's the plan for today?" Brian asked, after shooting a quick smile in Hentie's direction. "Are we going out on the truck? Serving hot beverages?"

"Technically, we're on vacation from the truck," I said, stifling a yawn behind my palm.

"I want to explore," Hentie said. "There's lots of places to visit in town, and the streets are clear, right?"

"It's not snowing today," I added in.

Smulder nodded. "I'll have to pass on coming along. I've got a couple of personal matters to attend to."

Hentie pet Barkington's head, but didn't ask what the personal matters were. My guess was that Brian would be talking to Special Agent in Charge Grant today. It had been months since we'd had a meaningful update about my status and whether it was safe for me to come out of hiding yet. Until the Crown Prince's "friends" were dealt with, there was no point in wondering. Essentially, the Crown Prince wouldn't stop until he'd punished me, but getting rid of him was out of the question. And brokering a deal to keep me safe would take a lot of resources, time and effort.

Which only made my desires to keep Hentie as a friend

more selfish. I swallowed a lump of emotion, a complex wad of different feelings, and got up. "Then it's settled. Let's get ready to go out on the town, Hentie."

"Have fun," Brian said. "And be careful."

We got dressed and met up, Barkington too, at the front of the Cakeville Chateau. The truck didn't take too long to warm up, and we were rattling down the street in no time. The scene next door was still cordoned off, though the body had been removed. The footprint was gone, likely covered by snowfall in the night.

"Let's go to the bookstore," I said. "Pay one of our suspects a visit."

"Who?"

"Celeste Chills."

"Ja, right. The woman who had that argument with Juniper before she died," Hentie said.

"That's the one. She got her bakery shut down by Juniper. The two clearly didn't like each other, and if we can figure out where Celeste was at around 11:00 p.m. on the night of the murder, we can either clear her or keep her as a person of interest."

Hentie made an indistinct noise as she looked out of the window. "And what about that other guy? The hiker we saw at the back of the inn?"

"Yeah, another person of interest to add to the list. Just

because he had permission to be there doesn't mean he's not suspicious. Particularly because he's a man," I said.

We'd checked his story with Edna, who'd confirmed that he was a good friend of hers, and she gave him free access to the woods behind her inn. Technically, the mountain and its surrounds were part of a preserve.

I directed the truck through the cozy streets of the town, their lampposts on and shimmering on the overcast day, and the store windows misty here or there, many of them with warm lights inside. The brick-faced stores had decorative signs with curling script. Benches along the paved sidewalks were covered in snow, but the cold weather didn't stop the Cakevillers from taking to the streets in their winter wear to shop, do business, or socialize with friends.

The book store, Chill's Books, was tucked away in a side street, between a florist's shop and a candle store. It was a miracle there weren't any bakeries in the street. We'd noticed an excessive amount of them on our drive over. In fact, there was one street, we hadn't gone down it yet, called "Baker's Row" that was packed with bakeries.

Hentie grabbed Barkington from where he'd been safely strapped into his crate, and we entered Chill's Bookstore. I stripped off my coat and hung it on a rack near the front. The bookstore was pleasantly warm, with a reading nook off to one side, shelves stocked with literature, and a circular counter in the middle of the space.

But the place was empty.

"Celeste?" I called out. "Hello, Celeste?"

"Over here!"

The call came from our left.

Hentie and I found Celeste on her knees, unpacking a box of books and stacking a display that faced the street.

"Good morn— Whoa." I took in the display.

Celeste smiled at me from where she kneeled among the books. "Do you like it?" She gestured with a book about an infamous serial killer. "I thought, you know, given the fact that Juniper was killed, folks might be interested to read more about other infamous serial killers." And then she held up the book beside her face and smiled. Creepy, since the man on the cover, who had been a serial killer, was smiling as well.

Not only had Celeste set up a display full of books about serial killers, but she'd decorated it with miniature Jack-o'-lanterns and bats and Halloween paraphernalia.

Barkington yapped. Hentie scratched her forehead. "Are you lekker in the kop?" she asked.

"Huh?"

"Are you feeling okay in your head?" Hentie asked. "Because this is a little bit psychopathic." She's said it, I was thinking it.

"What do you mean?" Celeste asked, and her expression shuttered. "This is a smart business decision. People come to Chill's for the spooks and thrills. This fits the bill."

"You don't think it's tone deaf?" Hentie asked. "A woman just died."

"A woman everyone hated," Celeste said, patting a book against her palm. "Are you here to buy something?"

"We wanted to check the place out," I said.

"Unless you're buying, you can leave. Now." The words were cold and direct.

Barkington barked his protest, patting his paws against Hentie's arm.

"Yeah, and no dogs allowed either."

Celeste glared at us all the way out of the store.

Eleven

That evening...

THERE WAS NOTHING WRONG WITH A HEALTHY intrigue about serial killers or true crime. I could relate, since I wanted to solve the case of the Halloween Killer, but to set up a display right after Juniper had been murdered? Suspicious.

In the privacy of my room at the Cakeville, after the others had retired after a dinner of butter burgers with cream puffs for dessert, I changed into a turtleneck sweater, put on my utility belt, and slipped contact lenses into my eyes.

The lenses were high-tech equipment that my grand-mother had helped design. With a couple of taps to my temple, I could cycle between modes. Night vision, infrared, and even a bluetooth setting that would connect to the camera of my mini-drone. Perfect for tonight's reconnaissance mission.

"If only Hentie could come with me," I murmured.

Hentie and I had spent the day going over our suspect list, chatting about the case and potential leads, and drinking our body weights in hot chocolate. No regrets. The Cakeville Chateau, and the town itself, specialized in sweet treats.

I didn't have an easy escape from my room—the windows opened outward, but the snow had packed against my window, and leaving a trail in the snow was a rookie mistake.

At half past ten, I left my room and walked down the hall. The dining area was blessedly empty. I'd half-expected Smulder to step out of a hidden nook and ask me what I was doing. But the inn was silent.

I unlocked the front door with my key then closed it and locked it again behind me. Five minutes later, I was in the ice cream truck, driving down the street, one hand on the wheel, the other fiddling with the dials on the dash to get the heat going.

Edna had told me that not only did Celeste run the bookstore, but she lived above it. And, apparently, the book store had once been the bakery that Juniper had shut down by reporting Celeste to a health and safety officer.

I parked down the street, then removed the silver pill from my fanny pack. I opened it, took out the fly-sized drone from within before tapping my left temple.

"Come on," I muttered. "Connect. Connect!" Even spies had issues with technology.

Finally, the view from the fly drone filled my vision. I picked up the cylindrical controller, rolled down the window, and then tossed the drone into the sky.

The drone's view was laid over my vision, which would have been dizzying if not for the training I'd done for scenarios like this. It was necessary for an operator to have complete control of their surroundings at all times. There was never a guarantee that I'd have back up to watch out for me while I did my investigative work.

I directed the drone toward the book store. The lights were off on the first floor, but the apartment above was illuminated. I drifted past the windows, searching for an entry point.

"Where are you?" I murmured.

The curtains were drawn. I couldn't see inside.

I flew the drone back down to the doors of the book

store then forced it through the keyhole and into the darkened interior.

It didn't escape my notice that Celeste had succeeded in finishing that display. The interior of the book store was hauntingly still, but I soon found the staircase near the back and flew up it.

I zipped through the keyhole of another door and into Celeste's apartment.

"Finally." The drone only had so much battery. I'd have to be quick.

I zipped through the upper floor, past Celeste, who was in the kitchen, eating cupcakes out of a box, scrolling on her phone. The layout was blessedly small. A bathroom, living room, kitchenette, and a bedroom.

The bedroom was neat, but Celeste had left her diary on the bed. And it was open, her bedside lamp providing warm light to read it by.

I hovered the drone over it and read.

Dear Diary,
She's finally gone. I never thought this day would come.
The fact that it took so long...
I don't know, I just feel like she got what was coming to her, and most of the

people in town agree. Especially after what she did to me. I never forgave her for it, and I never will.

They're going to have a funeral for Juniper, and I'm invited to attend, which is great, because I'll get to see Ben while I'm there. It's going to be so difficult to pretend everything is normal when I see him, but I'll do it. If his wife ever finds out about us, I have no idea what she'll do.

Apparently, she has a temper. Well, she can bring it on. If Penelope cared about Ben, then she would have paid more attention during their marriage. So, I guess she'll have to deal with it when he finally leaves her for me.

He told me that it's only a matter of timing. He can't leave her now that her sister is dead. He told me that she's distraught. That she'll never ever get over it, but that he thinks it will be a couple of months before we can be together.

Fine by me. I can wait a few months.

And then if she causes any more trouble, I'll deal with her. I wish that...

The writing continued on the next page, but I wasn't able to turn it because the drone didn't have that capability.

A shadow passed over the journal, and, just in time, I swept to the left, narrowly missing the end of a rolled up newspaper. Celeste swished the newspaper through the air, muttering something I couldn't hear, and glaring around.

That was my cue.

I directed the drone back out of the book store and down the street to my waiting palm. It landed, and I shut it down then carefully packed it back into its holder and slipped it into my utility belt. I had the answers I needed.

Not only was Celeste suspicious because of her hatred toward the victim, but she'd been having or rather, was having, an affair with the sister's husband. A clandestine affair and a murder? Could the two be related?

I'd already taken a snapshot of the journal entry, and I tacked it to the corkboard in my mind then studied it and the threads that connected everything.

The blurry image hadn't changed.

Was it possible that this case wasn't related to the Halloween Killer? Could this be a copycat? If that was the case, Celeste definitely fit the bill. She wanted revenge, she was embroiled in the family's affairs, and she had an interest in serial killers. She'd also had an outright argument with the deceased the night before.

But that wasn't enough evidence.

Something was missing.

Twelve

The next day...

HENTIE, BARKINGTON, AND I PILED INTO THE ICE cream truck bright and early, after our cream puffs and coffee, hopped up on sugar and caffeine. Except for Bark, of course, who was dressed in another snazzy sweater and knit booties today—Halloween themed with pumpkins and bats. Hentie was getting really good at knitting them.

"Where to?" Hentie asked, as she put on her seatbelt.

"I thought we could go check out the bakery that belonged to the victim," I said. "See what the fuss was about."

"Sounds good to me," Hentie said. "Do you think it was one of the people who hated her?"

"They're all suspects." I drove down the street, the food truck's engine purring. "But there's a couple of possibilities. Either, the killer is the Halloween Killer or a copycat who used the Halloween Killer's M.O. to try to pin the blame elsewhere."

Hentie sniffed. "But what is the Halloween Killer's motive? Do you think they're doing it just because they're sick in the head?"

I barked a laugh. I liked the way Hentie related to the world. "I'm not sure, but we can find out."

"Sheriff Stalz seems determined to solve the case. I bet he'll be happy if we give him some of the information we find."

"I'm surprised they haven't set up a hotline for tips yet," I said, "but I agree." For once, local law enforcement seemed competent and friendly. *Though, are they that competent if this case has gone unsolved for the last twenty years?* But with the new sheriff in charge, that might change.

A short drive through the town, shadowed by the gorgeous mountain, now capped with snow, brought us to Baker's Row. The street was actually called Point Street, but a swinging sign on a wrought iron post at the entry point declared otherwise.

"Baker's Row," I said. "Reminds me of Death Row."

Hentie pulled a face.

Bakeries populated the street, squished in side-by-side, with specials boards out front or signs tacked in their windows declaring the steep discounts. They were all pretty much in line with each other, apart from a bakery in the very center of "the Row."

The building was painted a bright blue, with a sign in curling script that read "Juniper's Delicacies". A huge notice had been put up on the inside of the clean glass window.

CLOSING SALE! ALL BAKED GOODS HALF OFF! TWO DAY ONLY SALE!

"Wow," Hentie said. "Is that normal? I wonder why it's closing? Juniper is dead, but, jong, isn't there anyone to take over?"

The way Juniper had talked about her bakery had made it seem that she was the most successful in town. And it did look welcoming, with a cute wooden front door and windows that gave a view of polished flooring with rugs and mismatched tables and chairs. It was the biggest building by far, and it dominated the street.

"Let's find out what's going on," I said, and parked the truck out front.

We grabbed Barkington from the crate then went inside.

The space bustled with activity. People gossiping and buying up the half-off baked goods. Servers rushed back and forth, wearing stress in the tense set of their shoulders. The smells were incredible.

I scanned the store then nudged Hentie. "There," I said. "In the corner."

Penelope, the Juniper lookalike, sat on her laptop, a pair of glasses perched on the end of her nose. Beside her was a handsome man with blond hair. He sat back, staring out of the front window with his arms crossed, pouting like a petulant child. That had to be Ben.

We walked over to them.

"Hello, Penelope," I said. "How are you?"

She removed her glasses and tapped her bottom lip with the earpiece. "Do I know you?"

"We met the other day at the Cakeville Chateau," I said.

"I screamed at you," Hentie put in, helpfully.

"Oh yeah, sure." She paused, then gave a small, uncomfortable chuckle that sounded like three hiccups. "Can I help you with something?"

"We noticed that the bakery is closing," I said. "And we wondered what had happened."

"She's decided to sell the darn thing." The husband sat forward. "Not that it matters what her partner thinks. She doesn't care about that."

"Now is not the time, Ben," Penelope snapped. "We're in polite conversation. Can't you keep your attitude to yourself for once?"

"Attitude?" Ben asked. "What are you, my mother? I'm not giving anyone attitude. I'm telling you, I think this is a bad financial decision. This place is practically a gold mine, prime real estate, and you want to sell?"

"And so what if I do?" Penelope asked. "Juniper left the bakery to me. To do with what I wish. Not to you. She didn't even like you, Ben."

"A fact I am well aware of, thank you very much. I've had to deal with your negative sister for over twenty years now," he said. "I'm glad she's gone."

"Do you think that bothers me?" Penelope asked. "I didn't particularly enjoy her company either. "You telling me that you'd prefer her dead doesn't faze me."

"Of course it doesn't," Ben said. "You're as cold-hearted as she was."

"I'm cold-hearted? You threw my sister's death in my face. If you wanted to discuss my inheritance, you should have asked, instead of throwing tantrums left and right."

"Tantrums?" Ben pushed up from the table. "You witch." And then he stormed off toward the counter.

He got curious glances as he passed people in the crowd.

"And that," Penelope said, "is why you always get a prenup. Take that as my sage advice."

"I'm sorry," I said, smoothly.

"That was awkward as heck." Hentie shifted Barkington in her arms. "Is he always like that?"

"He has been for years," Penelope said. "He keeps asking me for marriage counseling but what's the point? He's only asking so that he can weaponize it against me in our arguments. Anyway, as for the bakery, I have no interest in running it. I've never wanted to be a baker and there are plenty of others in town who would pay a huge amount of money for this space. So that's what I'm going to do. Get my money and get out."

"Good for you," I said, with a grin.

"Thanks," Penelope replied, and gave me a smile in return. "I'm sure there are plenty of people who think it's strange, me selling the place, but it's really not complicated. I don't have a passion for this type of thing, and my sister left me in charge. She also didn't say what I should do with the place. No instruction to keep it running, for instance. Anyway." She flapped her hand. "Lots to do today."

And that was our dismissal.

If she'd known that her husband was having an affair, how would she react? It wasn't my place to tell her, but perhaps...

Hentie led the way out of the bakery. "Did you see his feet, April?" she asked.

"What about them?"

"They were big."

I'd been invested in the conversation. I'd let that particular detail slide. But I hurriedly rifled through the memory until I found one of Ben rising from the table. Hentie was right. His feet were large, perhaps large enough to be those of a killer.

Thirteen

"SOMETHING STUCK WITH ME," I SAID, "ABOUT what Ben said at the bakery."

"Ja? What?" Hentie had grabbed us both mugs of hot chocolate from the kitchen, much to Niles' eternal unhappiness, and she placed mine on the coffee table in front of me.

We were set up in the enclosed porch at the back of the inn again, with the snowy trees for company, as well as Barkington, who was sleeping on an armchair next to mine. The inn's cat, Kerfuffle, had poked her flat pale face through the door, taken one look at us, and pranced off with her tail in the air, most unimpressed.

"Ben said that he'd been dealing with Juniper for over twenty years. What do you think that means?" I asked.

"They haven't been married for twenty years, surely. They looked around their forties or so?"

"They must have known each other way back. Maybe in high school?" Hentie sat down and brought out her phone. "There's a way to find out." And off she went, searching and tapping away on her phone.

I went back to my research as well.

Another article about the Cakeville Halloween Killer had drawn my attention.

The Victims of The Cakeville Killer: What Did They Have in Common?

Speculation has always surrounded the deaths in the Halloween Killer case in Cakeville, with many local citizens blaming them on those close to the victims or throwing suspicion on local law enforcement. The silence from the Casey County Sheriff's Department has been deafening, with Sheriff Stone refusing to comment on the deaths on account of it being an ongoing investigation.

With mystery swirling around the cases, it's worth taking a look at who the victims were, in an effort to discover what they might have in common, and how the Halloween Killer may have been identifying their victims.

The skin on the back of my neck prickled. There was something here that had brought that on. I reread the passage, but nothing jumped out at me immediately.

Belinda O'Toole, the first victim, was a grocery store clerk who had a sharp tongue but plenty of friends, as well as a boyfriend. She was an active member of society, but had gotten into arguments with townsfolk before her death, most of it surrounding the ownership of bakeries in Baker's Row. As a descendant of one of the original cranberry farmers of the town, she lost everything when the last farm shut down. She was last seen at a Halloween party on the night before Halloween at around 11:00 p.m., according to sources close to the case.

Gerald Stone, a librarian who threw stones at local children for making too much noise, had come from out of town and settled in Cakeville with his family in the 1980s. He was male, older, and was known for giving leeway with library fines. While he was grumpy about noise, he was kind to those who patronized the library. He didn't have any enemies and kept mostly to himself.

The most recent victims Bennie and Robert McCall, were brothers who were bee farmers and one of the chief suppliers of honey to local bakeries, inns, guesthouses, and restaurants in around Cakeville and Casey County. They were known for driving a hard bargain, and may have had enemies who were upset with how they dominated the honey market.

But what was the connection between them and the rest of the group? They were in their thirties, while librarian Gerald Stone, was in his sixties when his life was taken. Belinda was in her early twenties and female. It doesn't seem likely that the killer is picking victims based on their age or sex, so what is the connecting factor?

Could these innocent victims have encountered the victim in their everyday lives without realizing it?

I took a mental image of the information and saved it to my board.

The victims were so different, and if I added Juniper into the mix, she didn't fit either. Did that mean I had to rule out all Juniper's enemies and assume that she was killed by the Halloween Killer who had chosen her at random?

Interesting that Belinda had last been seen at 11:00 p.m. the night before her body was found. That was around the same time that the hiker, Wrenly, had last seen Juniper.

"They went to high school together," Hentie said. "I was right." She gave me a bright smile.

"Oh? Who did?"

"Most of the people in town who are around forty were in the same high school. Juniper, her sister, Penelope, the Sheriff, several of the deputies, Ben, and Celeste as well. That must be what Ben meant when he said he didn't want to deal with her any more because it had been over twenty years."

"What about Bennie and Roger McCall?"

Hentie checked. "Yeah, they were the year lower, but they were also in high school at around the same time."

"Belinda O' Toole?"

The timing would match up.

"Ja, she graduated in their class as well."

"Interesting," I said. "Very interesting."

I got up and paced back and forth, flicking my fingers as I went over the corkboard in my mind and the connections. I had three sections above the image of Juniper's body posed and set up as a witch, linking back to her. The three previous victims of the Halloween Killer.

"Do you think we can figure it out?" Hentie asked. "If the police haven't been able to and it's been so many years then—"

"We can figure it out," I said. "We have to put our heads together."

"All right."

I gnawed on my bottom lip.

"So, Juniper and Penelope were sisters, they didn't like each other," I said, then put up my palm. "Wrong thread. The killer struck out at several people who were in high school at the same time."

"Does that mean they were in high school too?" Hentie asked. "At the same time as the victims?"

"Maybe, but there was an anomaly. A librarian who was in their sixties. Why? Why was that person different to the others?" I murmured. "Let's see what we can find out about Mr. Gerald Stone. Sounds like there was a Sheriff Stone at one point. They might have been related, though I don't know if it's relevant."

Hentie scooched forward on her seat.

"As for Penelope and her husband, they might be involved because of the inheritance, but I doubt that it's them," I said. "They don't fit the profile. Besides, they've got their own marital issues to deal with."

"Maybe they'll work it out," Hentie said, absently. "Marriage is a marathon not a sprint. It takes a lot of work."

"Yeah, but you're lucky, Hentie. You have a nice husband who you get along with. Besides, he would never cheat on you."

"Cheat on me?" Hentie's gaze snapped to mine, her

green eyes narrowing. "Wat op aarde? Why would you even suggest that? Are you trying to give me a heart attack?"

"No, no," I said. "I was talking about Penelope and Ben." I stopped pacing and schooled my expression to neutral. *Idiot. Why did you say that?* I'd gotten too comfortable around Hentie. She had no idea that I'd done private reconnaissance. And she could never know.

I'd already told her too much the other day, giving her more information would endanger her life.

"Wat bedoel jy? What do you mean?" Hentie asked.

"Nothing. Don't worry about it."

Hentie set her phone down on the side table beside her cream-cushioned armchair. "No. What do you mean, April? Tell me."

Fourteen

"There's nothing to tell," I said. "It's just a lucky guess."

"Jinne, you must think I was born yesterday," Hentie replied, folding her arms and staring up at me. Her fluffy gray bun drooped to the side atop her head, tufts of hair framing her face. It would have looked comical if not for the thinning of her lips. "What do you know that I don't?"

Darn her being so perceptive. And darn me for being unwilling to gaslight her. I'd already told her that I wasn't who she thought I was, but I couldn't say more. And if she pushed, it would lead to... I didn't want to think about it.

"April?" Hentie prompted. Barkington yapped and stood up on all four paws staring at me.

They were ganging up on me.

"Come on, Hentie, you saw the way they argued. You don't think that they might have been having marital difficulties beyond—"

"I can understand that there are certain things you can't tell me about your personal life," Hentie said, "but I thought we were working on this case together."

"We are."

"Then did you find out information that made you believe Penelope's husband is having an affair?"

"I may have done some external research on my own."

Hentie pursed her lips. "On your own," she said. "Why? And why didn't you tell me about it?"

"I can't."

"You can't."

"No." I wet my lips. "Look, there are things you don't understand."

"Fine," Hentie said. "Fine. Lekker. But if you want us to work together on this case then you should involve me."

She didn't know that it was impossible for me to involve her in everything. "I'll tell you anything I find independently, but sometimes, it's not worth it because it's not something we can prove or that can be used as evidence."

"Then how on earth are you getting the information?"

"Word of mouth and other methods."

"Other methods?"

"Hentie, like I said—"

"You can't tell me," she said.

"Yeah."

Hentie rose from her seat and collected her hot chocolate.

"Where are you going?"

"I'm going to go build a snowman," she said. "Would you mind watching Barkington?"

"You don't want me to come with you?" I asked.

"No, thank you. I would prefer to be on my own. Listen, I know you can't tell me certain stuff, but that doesn't make me happy or make it easy for me. I like you, April. You're a fun person and a good friend, and I have enjoyed riding around on the truck with you and exploring, and especially solving mysteries, but I don't like secrets very much."

"I understand."

"I want some time alone." And then she walked off.

Barkington gave me an accusatory stare.

"What?" I asked. "Come on, I can't be that upfront."

He gave a muffled bark and settled down again. Would he ever forgive me? Would Hentie?

It was awful. All of it. Lying, being on the run, the fact that I could never tell Hentie who I was, and the realistic future that awaited me. Eventually, I would be called back to the NSIB, and I would start work again, and then the ice cream truck would be a thing of the past. Hentie and Bark would go back to their lives, and I would never see or hear from them again for their own safety.

I sat down and bowed my head, letting emotion overwhelm me for once.

I couldn't remember the last time I'd cried.

That was a lie. It had definitely been during my childhood when I'd lived with my mother. But as a woman, I had always kept my emotions under strict control.

Tears ran down my cheeks, and I let them. My shoulders shook, but I made no noise, not wanting to draw attention. Barkington whined at me, but I didn't go over to him for comfort. This was personal. And I needed to cry it out. It was the build up of everything.

The porch back door opened, and I hurriedly dried the underside of my eyes.

Smulder stepped out and stopped dead, his gaze fixing on my face.

"Not now, Oliver," I said. "I really don't want to talk."

"Then don't talk." He walked over and drew me out of the chair, then pulled me into his arms and rested my head against his chest.

I stiffened. "Brian," I murmured.

"Cry if you need to cry," he said. "Nobody said this would be easy, and you're only human."

Then the tears really came on, and I sobbed against him, clutching his shirt and tugging on it. Smulder stroked my back, and it helped. I didn't want it to help, but heaven knew, it helped, and I couldn't be angry at him for it.

Finally, we parted, and Brian produced a pack of Kleenex from his pocket and offered it to me.

"Thanks," I said, and dried my tears, dabbed my nose. "Sorry you had to see that."

"What? Why are you apologizing?"

"Because I cried in front of you?"

"That's normal, Delta," he murmured. "It's normal to cry. You realize that, right?"

I bit down on my bottom lip. Was it normal to cry? Yeah, of course. But I had internalized that doing it in front of other people was considered rude. *Ladies aren't meant to make other people uncomfortable with their emotions, Delta.* My mother's voice snapping me back to the past.

I reached out and grabbed hold of Smulder's hand. He squeezed it, keeping me here.

The last place I wanted to be was in my memories with my mother and her hate-filled voice.

"What is it?" Brian asked, closer than before. "What's wrong?"

"Nothing," I said. "I'm fine." I looked up at him, at his soft gaze, full of concern and so kind. The opposite of what I'd expected from him. That was the trust issues talking, obviously, but it was confusing.

Brian reached up and brushed my hair behind my ear, tucking it away gently. "If you need anything, just let me know, all right? If you want to talk about Hentie or about Grandpa or about—"

I rose onto my tiptoes and brushed a kiss over his lips.

Brian stiffened. "Are you sure you want—?"

I nodded.

He swept me into his arms and planted a toe-curling kiss on my lips, one that was neither chaste nor appropriate. My heart pounded in my chest, and I clung to him, hardly believing that I was allowing this to happen.

Barkington gave a warning bark, and Smulder and I sprang apart staring at each other. I touched my lips as the porch door opened and Hentie bustled out, carrying two mugs.

She stopped after a step. "Oh," she said. "Am I interrupting something?"

"Just checking the, uh—" Smulder said.

"Nope," I put in, at the same time.

We stared at each other then both cleared our throats and looked away.

"Excuse me," Brian said, dipping his head. "I was going to— Uh. I was going to go." And then he scooched past an amused-looking Hentie and out into the hall.

"Good thing I didn't try build the snowman in here," Hentie said, as she put down the mugs. "It would definitely have melted."

My cheeks flushed red hot.

Fifteen

THAT EVENING, BEFORE DINNER, I RETURNED TO my bedroom to freshen up and try not to think too much about what had happened with Brian. It was equal parts confusing and exciting, and I wasn't sure how to feel.

Hentie had been kind enough *not* to bring it up the entire afternoon while we went out to have a snack at a bakery. Our real task had been to pick up bits of information about Celeste, who had once owned a bakery, and about Juniper, her sister, and Ben. We hadn't gotten much except more insinuations that Ben wasn't faithful to his wife.

But a lack of loyalty didn't make him a murderer. Just a selfish person.

A scratching at my bedroom door made my heart leap, and I muttered under my breath at myself. Getting nervous wasn't part of my usual emotional repertoire, but neither was crying. Today was one of those days, apparently.

I opened the door and found the inn's cat, Kerfuffle, seated in the hall, almost regal in her assessment of me. Her flat white face showed nothing but disapproval, and she flicked her fluffy tail, yellow eyes unblinking.

"Can I help you, Queen Kerfuffle?" I asked.

She meowed at me, a tiny, haughty noise.

"Do you want to come in?"

Kerfuffle rose and sauntered off, in the direction of the back of the inn.

"Suit yourself," I said, and closed the door again.

I splashed water on my face, dried it, then put on mascara and lipstick—a soft pink that wasn't too over-done. *Since when do you care whether it's overdone or not? It's dinner. You're going to eat cream puffs and have a good time.*

A second round of scratching started at the door.

I grabbed my phone, slipped it into the pocket of my jeans then went to meet Kerfuffle. "What's wrong now, Queen Kerfuffle? Was my previous response not to your liking?"

Kerfuffle meowed. She was haughty, yes, but I could never bring myself to dislike a cat. Or any animal for that matter.

"I'm going to dinner," I said. "I can't let you hang out in my room, if that was what you wanted."

Another meow, this one more impatient. She rose and walked off down the hall again, stopping and circling back.

Is this cat trying to get me to follow it?

I took a step toward Kerfuffle, and she immediately gave an appreciative meow and pittered down the hallway on her fluffy white paws. I followed her, and she led me to the back porch. I opened the door and the cat leaped onto an armchair and then onto the sill that looked over the back yard. Promptly, she settled her white butt and started licking her paws.

"Really?" I asked. "That was it? You wanted someone to open the door for you?"

Her Majesty Kerfuffle didn't grace me with a response. I turned to go, but instinct stopped me. I walked to the window beside Kerfuffle who purred and presented herself for pets.

I stroked her furry head.

Outside, dusk had come, a fading haze, and the recently fallen snow laid white over the yard, except where it was disturbed by a trail of footprints. Large footprints. That led around the side of the inn to the exterior porch door and stopped.

"Kerfuffle," I whispered. "You're a genius."

She meowed in a way that sounded like, "I knew that. Glad you finally figured it out."

I took a snapshot of the foot prints and added them to the corkboard, then walked to the back door and looked out. I tested it, but it was locked. The footprints trailed away into the trees.

There were a few options. Either Wrenly, the hiker, had come back to the inn and tried to come inside to see Edna then decided to go on a hike, or the killer had been here. Of course, there were other men in town who might have paid the inn a visit, but to come around the back, try the door, and then leave through the woods? That was specific. And strange.

The forest was pressed against the mountain and part of the preserve. Parts of the mountain were impassable and dangerous, especially in the snow, and there were rangers who cared for the area.

A ranger. A park ranger. That's who it could be.

Did Edna know any rangers? I'd have to ask.

I walked back into the inn proper, leaving Kerfuffle to clean her paws and celebrate her victory. Hentie and Smulder sat together at a table against the wall, near the fireplace. They chatted, and Hentie laughed at something Smulder had said. He caught sight of me, and his face went slack, his eyes wide, before he broke eye contact.

"April, dear," Edna said, appearing in the kitchen

doorway. Tonight, she'd changed into a sparkling tiara. "I thought you were going to miss us this evening. Come on, now, sit down and enjoy the cream puff entree."

I'd had enough cream puffs for an army, but I would never say no to more of them. "Edna," I said, and went over to her. "Do you have any park ranger friends?"

"Me? No, not really. I'm not the spelunking type. I like to keep my feet dry and my make-up flawless." She gestured to her face. "Why do you ask?"

"I found a trail of footprints leading up to the back door and then away again into the woods. I thought it might be your friend, Wrenly."

"Wrenly? Oh no, he wouldn't come out here today. He always asks me first. Always. Such a gentleman, and so unfortunate about what happened with his previous business," she said, leaning in and lowering her voice. It was still loud enough for everyone in the room to hear what was being said. Especially since they'd quieted to hear the exchange.

"What happened?" I asked.

"It closed down, of course. But he wasn't as upset about it as we thought he'd be," Edna said. "He told me, personally, that he didn't think a bakery like his would survive in Cakeville. He was too rustic and focused on bread rather than cakes and sweets. He had a plan to create a line of breads and baked goods specifically for hikers."

"He owned a bakery."

"That's right. Wrenly's Loaves and Sundry. I was sad for him when it closed down. He's such a nice man. I don't see—"

"How old is Wrenly, Edna?" I asked.

"Oh, he's in his forties, I think," Edna said. "But that hair and beard might give you the impression that he's older than his years. He's certainly wiser. I still can't believe that he didn't get mad at Juniper when she had him shut down." She straightened her tiara. "Juniper didn't like anyone who competed with her, and Wrenly was gaining popularity. Until she had *The Cakeville Chatter* run an article about how bad stoneground flour is for the digestive system. Which isn't true, of course, but the damage was done. And then article after article came out about poor Wrenly, and it was over before it properly got off the ground."

Propaganda. The woman had used propaganda. The more I learned about Juniper, the less I liked her, but she hadn't deserved murder.

A bell tinkled from the kitchen, and Edna laughed. "I almost talked through supper." And off she went toward the kitchen doors to harangue a tired Niles.

Sixteen

THE NEXT MORNING, THE PLAN WAS TO GO PAY Wrenly a visit. We hadn't exactly asked him about his past or his relationship with Juniper, but I was still suspicious, and so was Hentie. Edna had obligingly given us his address.

He lived in a log cabin on the outskirts of town, on the opposite side to the mountain. The cabin was at the end of a dirt road, with plenty of foliage and trees and a view of the mountain. It didn't border the preserve, however.

"This guy should have told you about Juniper," Hentie said. "He left it out on purpose."

"I don't know about that," I said. "It wasn't like I asked him specific questions about his relationship with her. People don't offer up private information willy-nilly.

They don't have to. Would you like to relive past traumas all the time."

Hentie harrumphed but didn't dispute my words.

We took the long dirt road up to the cabin and parked beside a truck that was weather-beaten and well used. The kind of truck that could withstand the elements and was an old friend at this point. The snow had been cleared away from it and the road we'd arrived on, but the rest of the lawn was layered thick.

"What a nice place," Hentie said, leaning forward and straining against her seatbelt to get a better view.

And she was right. The log cabin had floor-to-ceiling windows coated in a film to keep out the cold and prying eyes. The door was arched with a thick wrought iron handle, and smoke drifted from a chimney above the house.

"Looks like he's home," I said.

"What are we going to say to him?" Hentie asked. "We can't ask him whether he killed her or not."

"Don't worry," I said. "I have an idea. Grab Barkington out of the back and let's head up there."

Hentie unclipped her seatbelt and got out. The three of us met up on the porch—empty except for a telescope that was clear of frost or ice or any sign that it had been out in the inclement weather. Had Wrenly put it out recently?

And how could he afford such a nice house if his business had failed?

I knocked on the front door.

Several deep barks rang out from within the cabin, and Barkington yapped a response.

"It's okay, Blaffies," Hentie cooed.

The door opened, and Wrenly's smiling, bearded face appeared. It was lined with wrinkles and tanned from hours spent in the sun and outdoors. Years worth of a life well-lived. He nudged a dog—a Rottweiler with slobbery jowls—to the side. "Relax, Hen. Relax!"

Hen the dog. Interesting. Cute, even.

"Sit! Sit. Come on, girl, sit." Wrenly held out a palm, and the dog sat down, quirking an expressive brown eyebrow at her master. "Sorry about that," Wrenly said. "She gets excited when somebody comes to visit. You know how it is." He nodded toward Barkington. "Though looks like you trained 'im real good."

"Who Barkington?" Hentie laughed. "No, Bark is a menace." And indeed, Barkington squirmed and yapped to be free of Hentie's arms. She scolded him but finally let him down.

Barkington ran over to the Rottweiler and began sniffing her feet. Hen rolled over onto her back right away, submitting to Bark's attention.

"That's something," Wrenly said. "Never seen her act like this before."

"Barkington is a natural leader," Hentie replied proudly.

Barkington had also put himself in significantly dangerous positions over the months we'd been traveling together, and he tended to bark at the wind, but I admired Hentie's loyalty and her willingness to praise him.

"What can I do for you lovely ladies?" Wrenly asked with another of those toothless smiles.

"This is going to seem out of the blue," I said, "so forgive me this question, but we're worried about our safety?"

"Come in outta the cold." He opened the door wider and we entered the cabin. It was as cozy as it had looked from outside—a warm hallway that smelled of baking bread and had wooden floors that creaked underfoot.

The dogs ran ahead, barking and playing, Barkington clearly infatuated with Hen already.

We entered the living room, which had a view of the open plan kitchen, and took seats on comfy leather couches.

"Can I take your coats?" Wrenly asked.

"We're not going to stay long," I replied.

"All right, what can I help you with?"

"Well, after the murder," I said, "we've been feeling

jumpy. Did you hear that there was a footprint found at the scene?"

"I didn't, no," Wrenly said, and went over to the fire. He stoked it, stabbing the viciously sharp end of the poker into the flaming embers.

"A man's footprint. A large one. I noticed that you left large prints at the back of the inn," I said, then paused to assess his reaction.

"All right?"

"But this morning when we woke up, we spotted more footprints leading toward the back of the inn and away into the forest. We wondered if you'd been out at the Chateau, because then we'd know it was you and not the killer."

Wrenly pulled a face. "I'm afraid it wasn't me. I've been home for days now, baking bread."

"Bread?" Hentie prompted. "Why?"

"I enjoy it. But I have a business that sells artisanal bread to some of the local restaurants."

The same business that had closed down? "We heard that your bakery was..."

"Closed?" Wrenly asked. "Oh yeah, that's true. The storefront closed down after bad press, but I started operatin' from home. Thought it was the better option. Though, that's about to change for good." And he broke into another of those gleeful smiles.

"Why's that?" I asked.

"You know how that, uh, Juniper went and got herself killed?"

"Sure do," I said. "That's kind of why we're here, remember?"

"Right, of course. Anyway," Wrenly said, swooping the hot poker through the air. Hentie ducked and winced even though he was nowhere near the couch. "I figured it's best to make hay while the sun shines, so I bought her old bakery."

"Juniper's bakery?"

"That's the place. Got it from her sister for a steal. Seemed like she wanted to get rid of it, though I don't know why. That's prime real estate, that place is." Wrenly set the poker down and spread his arms. "And now, Wrenly's Loaves and Sundry will open up again, rebranded, and without anyone to bring it down."

"We heard that Juniper—"

"Yeah, she did," Wrenly said, as if he could read my mind. "She tried her best to get me put out of business, but it didn't work. If I've said it once, I'll say it again. I'm not sorry she's gone. I'm sorry she died in the way she did, though."

"It's got to be the Halloween Killer," Hentie said.

"Maybe. Maybe," Wrenly replied. "Who knows?"

We thanked him for his time and took a whiny Barkington—he wanted to stay and play with his new friend—back out to the truck.

"What do you think?" Hentie asked, once we were back inside the ice cream truck's temperate interior.

I turned the key in the ignition. "I think everyone in this town has something to hide, and Wrenly is no exception."

And I didn't believe a word he'd said, apart from the purchase of the bakery.

Seventeen

The next morning...

WRENLY HAD MADE MY SUSPECT LIST. I'D already tacked that image of him to my corkboard, and I stood in my bedroom, eyes closed, examining it in full. All the little connections back to Juniper and to the Halloween Killings.

The same age group apart from one man. Why? What had Gerald Stone done to become a target of the killer. What had the others done, for that matter?

I inhaled, held the breath for four counts, and then released it again.

Wrenly.

Celeste.

Penelope.

Her disloyal husband, Ben.

The cross-section of the Halloween Killer's profile, male, vengeful, average height, with the evidence presented about Juniper's death. She had last been seen on the night before her body was found at the Chateau. And most of the suspects had been in proximity.

But if the killer was male, that only left me with Wrenly and Ben. Unless, of course, there was someone else who might have been involved.

If I could just see that darn blurry image in my mind!

Footsteps rustled in the silence outside my bedroom window, and my eyes snapped open.

Wrenly walked past the side of the house, a backpack on his back, humming under his breath. Apparently, he'd changed his mind since yesterday. That or he'd arrived to cover his tracks.

I sprang to action, grabbing my coat and my fanny pack full of spy tools and hurrying out of my room. It was early, around six in the morning, and still dark. Hentie and Barkington were probably sleeping in. I ran down the hall, my steps as quiet as I could make them, and onto the back porch in time to spot Wrenly walking toward the woods.

I clunked on my boots—I'd left a pair by the back door

the day before—and followed him out into the snow. A fence bordered the preserve, but it was easy to climb over. A light dusting fell from the heavens, and it was icy cold, but Wrenly wasn't difficult to follow. His tracks were clear, as was the flashlight he carried through the woods at the early hour.

I moved, catlike, into the trees, hiding behind trunks as he continued down the trail.

Wrenly hummed a song, like he didn't have a care in the world, and directed the flashlight up the path ahead. "Off to find treasure in the mountains," he sang. "Off to spend the day in nature. The best way to spend any day."

Treasure?

Not this again. I'd had enough of messages in bottles and treasures.

The air beneath the trees was biting, and the tip of my nose was cold. Thankfully, my coat had a hood, and I pulled it up, tucking my hands into my pockets as I followed him. I'd been in the Siberian wilds, I'd survived horrible winters, but that didn't make this any easier.

Wrenly continued for a half an hour, swerving left and right. Thankfully, he stayed on the trail, which would make getting back to the Chateau easy, if I had to do it alone.

Finally, he reached the base of the mountain and promptly disappeared.

I stopped dead.

What on earth?

Where had he gone?

Wrenly had entered the clearing ahead of me, the beginnings of light now creeping across the ground, and simply vanished. The area he'd disappeared was rocky, with a small iced over pool of water, and snow-covered ground beside it.

Were my eyes deceiving me? I narrowed them, scanning the side of the cliff face. It was steep here, but further along the curve, it evened out and became a climbable bank, with shrubs and a smattering of trees.

He hadn't gone that way, though, or along the mountain to the west. So where on earth—?

A flash of light caught my attention, and I circled through the trees, changing my perspective.

Ah. That explains it.

I couldn't see it in the early morning light before, but there was a crack in the cliff face. Two jagged edges formed a gap that was big enough to fit a man of Wrenly's size.

A cave. Wrenly had gone inside a cave.

He'd mentioned spelunking the other day, but I'd dismissed it. Or thought it wasn't relevant.

Had I been wrong?

I crept toward the cave opening, listening hard. The

scattering of rocks, and Wrenly's soft humming came from within.

I squeezed through the gap, practicing my breathing, and entered the inside of the mountain. There was nothing like the claustrophobia of a cave, but the tight squeeze soon opened out into a cavern with stalagmites that looked as if they'd been standing for eons. The ones closer to the front of the cave were worn or broken.

Wrenly's light flashed much further back, and his voice echoed in the dark.

I couldn't afford to turn on my phone's flashlight or he'd spot me, but the meager light at the front of the cave didn't penetrate deep enough.

Now what?

"Off to find my treasures, to camp, and find my home," Wrenly sang.

I followed his voice. Feeling my way forward and placing my feet carefully. The ground was uneven, and the going was slow.

Wrenly's singing grew closer with every step. It seemed he had stopped.

His flashlight came into view, as well as the silhouette of him bending down and fiddling with something. "My treasures, their treasures, everyone's treasures," he sang.

The man had better stick to baking bread, because there was no future in music for him.

"And we'll tell them all the truth when we have to," Wrenly sang. "Because that will be the way to go. But if we try too hard—" There was a flare of a match, and Wrenly bent over a crude firepit. A moment later, more light flared.

His back was to me.

And behind him was a narrowing of the cave— another tight squeeze.

"They'll have to come here soon enough," he whispered. "And when they do, they'll pay for what they've done." No singing this time.

And that was just about enough for me. I stepped into the growing circle of firelight and chopped my hand down on the side of his neck against the vagus nerve. Wrenly toppled, but I caught him before he hit his head and lowered him down beside the fire.

A stack of firewood sat nearby. I grabbed a few logs and fed them into the fire, then rummaged through Wrenly's pack. He had a knife, rope, and bottles of water, a packed lunch, and a worn copy of *The Hobbit* by J.R.R. Tolkien. Good choice in literature, I'd give him that.

I secured his arms and legs, then sat him upright beside the fire, balancing him so that he was propped up against a rock.

It was cold in the cave, but nowhere near as cold as it had been near the opening, where the wind and snow had gusted inside. I fed the fire, then sat down with Wrenly's book and rifled through it. He had made notes in the columns, scribbling about dragons and treasures and the heroics of the party.

I set the book aside, folded my arms, and waited for my suspect to wake up.

Eighteen

Wrenly's eyelids fluttered open, and he groaned. "What the—? What?"

"Hi," I said. "How are you?"

"Help!" Wrenly screamed. "It's the Halloween Killer! Somebody help me, please!"

"Stop that," I said. "I'm not the Halloween Killer, Wrenly. And if I was, don't you think I would have killed you already instead of waiting for you to wake up?"

He wet his top lip, licking at the whiskers that had grown over it. "I don't believe you."

"Wrenly—"

"Help! Please help me!"

"Wrenly, if you don't quiet down, I'm going to have to make you," I said.

But the screaming didn't stop.

I let him yell while I rooted around in his backpack. I found a handkerchief, and I promptly tied it around his mouth and gagged him.

"There," I said. "I can talk to you and actually think about what I'm saying." I didn't plan on letting Wrenly remember anything of this encounter. "Mr. Holmes, I understand that this must be alarming for you, but not half as alarming as listening to you sing a song about treasure and capturing people. If you're wondering how I found you, it's because I followed you here. You were loud. Bear that in mind when you go hiking in future." Maybe that helped scare off the wildlife.

Wrenly frowned at me, but some of the fear drained out his face.

"I'm not the Halloween Killer. I thought you were. That's the reason you're tied up and at my mercy," I said. "Are you willing to talk to me without yelling?"

He didn't nod or shake his head.

Wrenly clearly needed more motivation, or an explanation as to why I was interested or how I'd overpowered him. "I'm a Special Agent undercover," I said. "And I'm working on the case of the Halloween Killer."

His eyebrows rose.

"Does that help?"

A slow nod.

"Good. I'm going to remove your gag, and we're going

to talk. I need you to answer my questions truthfully," I said. "And if you don't, I'll know."

Wrenly gulped.

I came forward and removed the gag then dropped it on top of his pack.

"Now, we can talk," I said, and crouched down beside the fire. "Wrenly, tell me why you were singing about treasure and taking revenge on people."

"I wasn't singing about revenge," he whispered. "I—I found something. Here. In this cave."

"What did you find?"

"A stash of items. At first, I thought they were just a kid's toys, but then I realized that someone was coming here a whole lot. They made the fire pit. And one time I came here, I heard noises in the dark. I left before they got me."

"Got you?"

"Whoever it is, I think... I think it's the killer."

"What makes you so sure?"

"Cos' of the items they've stashed away. I can't tell you. I've gotta show you."

I considered it.

I had plenty of tools in my utility belt to take him down if he decided to make any rash moves, but it was] dangerous.

"If you think it's the killer's stash, why didn't you report it to the police?" I asked.

"Why would I? The cops don't do nothing in this town. I told them about Juniper and the stuff she did to me, and they laughed it off. They're corrupt."

"But there's a new sheriff."

"And so? That don't change the situation," Wrenly said. "One of the last sheriffs didn't even care and his son was one of the victims, for Pete's sake. Then again, he was old as heck, so maybe he didn't realize what was going on."

I got up and went over, lifting Wrenly's knife from where I'd placed it next to his pack. "All right," I said. "I'll cut you free so you can show me the stash, but play ball. Got it?"

"You're with the FBI. I'm not going to mess with nobody from the FBI." He hesitated, eyes narrowing. "Say, how do I know you're FBI at all? Where's your badge?"

"Back at the Chateau," I said, crouching in front of him. "The way I see it, you have two choices, Mr. Holmes. You can believe me, show me the stash, and move on with your life. Or you can choose not to trust me, and get in trouble with law enforcement for obstructing justice. Already, you not reporting this 'killer's stash' to the police is a huge problem."

Wrenly swallowed. "All right, all right."

I cut the ropes on his feet and hands, then helped him up.

"Thanks," he said, then massaged his neck. He grabbed his phone and turned on the flashlight again. "It's this way." And then he led me toward the narrow squeeze. I followed him in, pushing between the rocks, the knife held at my side.

But Wrenly didn't spin around or try any funny business. He led me deeper into the cave, took a left, and continued along a wall, squeezing through another small opening.

Finally, he stopped and pointed. "There," he said. "In that corner."

It was curved rather than sharp-edged, so it barely classified as a corner, but Wrenly and I walked toward a gathering of items tucked away in the cave. I switched on my flashlight on my phone and crouched down, Wrenly joining me in the act.

There were several things laid out.

A folded up apron that was worn and faded, bearing the logo of "The Cakeville General Store".

A hardcover book that I was sure was from the library. I didn't touch it, regardless, in case there was trace evidence on the cover.

A metal honey dipper lay atop the apron, neatly placed.

And finally, a bracelet, that was most likely Juniper's.

These were the trinkets from the Halloween Killer, hidden in the cave. And Wrenly had found them.

"When did you first stumble on this?" I asked, turning my head.

"I found it a few weeks ago. Before the bracelet was placed with the other stuff. At first, I didn't get it. I thought it was a homeless person who needed a place to stay. Turned out, it wasn't."

I nodded. "Let's go back to the fire. I'm going to inform the authorities about this."

"If you really think that's the best idea," Wrenly said, sounding skeptical. "I don't think the cops will care. They'll cover it up. This stuff wasn't that hard to find. How come they haven't tried to check the preserve or the caves or any of it?"

I didn't answer him.

We squeezed back the way we'd come and Wrenly put his stuff back in his backpack. He sat down at the fireside. "Now what?"

I pointed to the entrance of the cave and he turned his head to stare at it. "We need to make sure that nobody disturbs the scene."

While he was distracted, I opened my fanny pack and removed a cylinder. I pressed it to my lips then blow-darted him in the neck. The solution inside would knock him out and give him temporary amnesia.

It was the only blow dart of its kind I had and I'd been saving it for a special occasion.

Wrenly keeled over sideways beside the fire. He would be warm, and he would wake up in the next ten minutes. I made sure he was moved out of harm's way, then headed for the exit, my jaw set.

Nineteen

I HIKED BACK ALONG THE TRAIL, HEEDLESS OF whether Wrenly would notice my passage. He'd already trampled the snow, and I had bigger problems to worry about. What he'd found in the cave proved that the footprints we'd seen in the snow the other day had belonged to the killer.

Which told me that they had definitely been wearing mens size 13 shoes, and were most likely a man, and that the murderer wasn't a random hater of Juniper's or a person she'd wronged. Rather, it was the Halloween Killer.

I'd taken a mental image of the trinkets the killer had left behind, but the blurry picture in my mind hadn't cleared yet. Something was missing.

The connection to Gerald Stone, the librarian, was puzzling to me.

I needed more information about those who'd gone to high school with the victims.

And then there was Penelope's husband. He hadn't been at the party, as far as I could remember, but there was no evidence that the killing had happened near the Chateau. He had the right size feet, and was strong enough to set up scenes. He'd also gone to the same school as the others.

That graduating class seemed to be the clue.

I reached the back of the inn and entered the porch, hurriedly kicking off my boots and locking up behind myself. I hung up my coat on the rack, then entered the inn, my mind ticking and whirring non stop.

A man.

But why?

What was the connection between the victims and the killer? What was the motive? Could Wrenly have lied to me? It wasn't like I could afford truth serum. When I'd talked to Gamma Mission about extra tools to take with me, truth serum was the one thing she couldn't give me.

Wrenly could have lied.

I needed proof.

I walked down the hallway thinking about it and dull chatter reached my ears from the dining area. It was almost time for breakfast, so I entered the room to find Hentie. She wasn't in our usual spot beside the fire.

Instead, Edna, wearing several beaded necklaces that clicked when she moved, sat in an armchair across from Celeste, who was crying and shaking her head.

Curious, I went over to our favorite table. Niles came out of the kitchen with a pot of coffee a few moments later and brought it over to me. With a mug of coffee in hand, I sipped idly and fiddled on my phone, pretending not to listen in on the conversation.

"My dear, it might seem impossible now, but you must realize things will get better," Edna said, her tone kind. "It was never a good idea to get involved with a married man."

Another sniffle from Celeste. "I thought he loved me. He told me that he was going to leave his wife for me, and now, he doesn't want to. How can he be like that? After everything we've shared. I poured my heart out to him."

"I understand," Edna said. "But you must see that he was only using you, dear. It's time for you to move on. Maybe, you should focus on yourself first before you go back to dating. And when you do go back to dating, stay away from those men who are unavailable."

"But I love him."

Edna sighed, beleaguered. I didn't blame her.

"I love him. He has to see sense."

"You love the person that he told you he was, not the person he actually is. For heaven's sake, what do you think would have happened if he had wound up leaving his wife and marrying you?"

"We would have been happy."

"Until another woman came along who interested him."

"It wasn't like that," Celeste said, her voice tight. "He loved me and I love him!"

"All right, dear. All right. You don't need to get upset. Everything will be fine."

"How can it ever be fine, when—"

A knocking banged at the closed front doors of the Chateau. Edna excused herself from the conversation, and Celeste's unhappy sobs were the backdrop to another few sips of coffee. Hentie entered the dining area with Barkington in her arms and gave me a wave.

I smiled as she joined me. Niles was just on his way over to pour her first cup of coffee when Sheriff Stalz entered the living room.

Edna walked alongside him, beads clattering, wringing her hands. "Are you sure, Sheriff? It seems like such a—"

"I'm sure," he said.

We watched him, turning in our chairs like the other guests in the dining room. Sheriff Stalz stopped beside where the miserable Celeste sat, wiping underneath her eyes, repeatedly. Stalz cut an impressive figure in his uniform, scratching fingers through the thatch of dark hair on his too big-head.

"Celeste Chills," Stalz said.

"Hello, Sheriff? What do you need? I was in the middle of a private conversation with Edna, and I—"

"I'm afraid you won't have time to finish that conversation," Stalz said, and puffed out his chest, exceedingly proud. He projected his voice so it carried through the dining room. "Miss Celeste Chills, you are under arrest for the murder of Juniper Berger. Please stand up with your arms out, facing away from me."

"W-What? Are you out of your mind?" Celeste asked, wide-eyed. "This is impossible. I didn't—"

"Stand up, please, Miss Chills."

Celeste's gaze flicked from the sheriff's face to Edna's, and then to the others in the room, all staring at her. With tears in her eyes, she rose and turned around as Stalz had told her. He put her in cuffs then marched her out.

The guests were shocked by the sudden arrest, but a smattering of applause followed the sheriff.

Edna stared dead ahead, almost as if she were in a trance.

"Edna?" I asked. "Are you all right?"

She shook herself and put up a smile. "Yes, dear. I just... I can't believe that happened. Never in all my years has the calm of my inn been invaded like that. I was sitting there," Edna said, pointing to her empty armchair at the fireside. "Right there. With a murderer. And I didn't even know it." She clutched both hands to her chest, dramatically. "Thank goodness Sheriff Stalz came in and saved me before she decided to take her temper out on me. Did you hear her? She started yelling at me about that affair she was having. I bet she mistook Juniper for Penelope, and that was why she killed her."

An interesting theory, except for the fact that I was sure that the killer was a man. And I doubted Celeste had gone spelunking around the inn in shoes too big for her. She was slight and had been shorter than Juniper, so how had she hauled the body from wherever she had allegedly killed Juniper to the crime scene?

It didn't add up.

Hentie muttered under her breath as Edna strode toward the kitchen doors to get started on breakfast.

"What do you think?" I asked Hentie.

"It's not right," Hentie murmured. "After the stuff we read online and the extra research we did. I don't believe it, April. Why did he arrest her? Like Celeste said, it's impossible."

I agreed with Celeste and Hentie.

Impossible.

Twenty

HENTIE HAD A PHONE CALL WITH HER HUSBAND after breakfast, so we didn't get much time to talk about Celeste's arrest or what I'd discovered in the cave with Wrenly. Instead, I grabbed my laptop from my cozy bedroom and went to the back porch while she had her chat.

Smulder hadn't talked to me much since our kiss, and whenever we spotted each other in the hall, we turned around and walked away from each other. It was juvenile, but neither of us was ready to deal with what had happened.

It suited me because he'd pretty much left me to my own devices. And my investigations.

I sat down with the laptop and opened it, trying to temper the urge to rush off and start asking questions, particularly of Penelope's husband, Ben, who was now my main suspect.

But there's a missing piece to the puzzle.

If it had been that simple, if it was just Ben or just Wrenly, that image in my mind would have cleared, and I would have my answer. I would already be working to expose the killer and have them arrested.

Which made me wonder what Sheriff Stalz and the sheriff's department found on Celeste? They had to have hard evidence to get a warrant for her arrest, right?

I typed in the name "Gerald Stone."

Articles about him popped up, all of them linking back to the Halloween Killer, but none of them pointing out anything new apart from the fact that he'd pelted kids with rocks outside the library.

Not the friendliest guy around, but not worthy of being murdered. Nobody was.

I scrolled through the results then clicked through to the next page.

Crunching on the snow outside drew my attention. Wrenly was back, looking a little groggy but unconcerned as he trooped past the side of the inn. He spotted me inside, lifted a gloved hand. I returned the greeting.

Looked like the blow dart had worked its magic.

Article after article covered the Halloween Killer and Gerald Stone's death, but none of them told me what I wanted. Who was he? How was he actually connected to the other killings? He was too old to have gone to high school with the other victims.

At the bottom of the third page of search results, I found a link to an obituary in the Cakeville Chatter's online website.

Stone, Gerald Walter

February 15th, 1947 - October 31st, 2007

Gerald Walter Stone, 60, of Cakeville, Wisconsin, died October 31st, 2007.

Gerald, son of ex-sheriff, Dayton Stone, passed away on October 31st due to unforeseen circumstances. Though he didn't have any family, Gerald will be missed by the graduates of Cakeville High School, where he served as the school librarian, as well as community members of Cakeville, who frequented the Cakeville Public Library in the years before his death. An avid reader, Gerald brought his love of books to those closest to him and was passionate about keeping the peace.

He enjoyed reading, fishing, and the occasional hiking trip in the Cakeville Nature Preserve. He will be sorely missed by the community.

Services will be held this Friday at the Cakeville Funeral Home at 03:00 p.m.

I couldn't help wondering who had taken out the obituary in the paper in the first place. It had to be a family member or a friend.

But more interesting was the fact that he had been a school librarian. I had my connection.

Every single victim had been connected to the Cakeville High School and the graduating class of 2002. And that meant that the killer had either been a teacher at the school or a part of the class.

The interior porch door slid open, and Hentie emerged.

"Thank goodness you're here," I said. "I've got a lot to tell you. We need to go pay Penelope and Ben a visit. I think I've— Hentie? What's wrong?"

"April," Hentie said, cheeks wan. "Oh, April." She took a stumbling step forward.

I put my laptop down on the side table and rushed over to my friend. "Hentie?"

"I—I—" And then she burst into tears.

I threw my arms around her and caught Hentie before she collapsed. Barkington let out a flurry of barks from the open sliding door. I patted Hentie's back. "What's going on?" I guided her to a chair and sat her down. "Hold on, I'll get tissues." I rushed down the hall to my room and burst into it, then grabbed a pack of Kleenex from my bedside table. The same pack that Brian had given me when I'd been weeping.

I rushed back to Hentie and handed her a tissue. She blew her nose noisily. Tears running down her cheeks and her gray messy bun wobbling as she cried.

"What's going on, Hentie?" *Who do I need to kill?*

"I—I'm so sorry, April."

"About what?"

"I have to leave," she said.

My heart sank like a stone. "What do you mean? Why?"

"Franklin is sick. He's sick, and he needs my help."

Barkington howled and pittered over, turning in a circle and demanding to be lifted up. I placed him in Hentie's lap, and she hugged him.

"I'm so sorry, Hentie. I'm so sorry. Do you know what it is."

She nodded.

"Is it bad?"

Another nod.

"Is it... ?"

"Of the stomach," she whispered.

"Oh, Hentie." I hugged her tight. "Oh, Hentie, I'm so sorry."

We embraced for a while until, finally, she drew back, drying her tears. She rolled her shoulders, strength and color returning to her face. "I won't let anything happen to him," Hentie said. "I have to go to him and find out how bad this situation is."

"Do you want me to come with you? I can drive us all the way to Texas. We can leave right now. I don't even care. I'll do it," I said.

Hentie gave me a watery smile. "No, we've both worked hard on this Halloween Killer thing," she whispered, glancing toward the door. "You need to see it through. I'm going to rent a car and drive to the nearest airport. But I need to ask you a favor."

"Anything."

"Please look after my little Blaffies while I'm gone?"

"Of course," I said. "Anything for you. And I'll keep Barkington safe."

"Ek weet. I know, April," she said. "You are the strongest and scariest woman I've ever met. Nothing bad will happen to Blaffies while he's with you." She hugged her puppy dog close to her chest. "The minute I know what's going on, I'll call you."

"How about I come to you?" I asked. "You let me know what's going on, and I'll drive down to Texas. Oliver will come with me."

"That would be wonderful," Hentie said. "Maybe it's not as bad as I think! Maybe I'll be able to fly back soon, but I need to be with my husband, April. I hope you can understand."

"Hentie, you don't need to explain anything to me." I took a breath. "When are you leaving?"

"I'm going to go pack my bags right away, and then I'll get a car."

"I can help you," I said.

"Thank you, April. You're a wonderful friend. I'm sorry we fought earlier in the week. I should have been more patient."

"No, Hentie, you were right. I should have trusted you more."

Together, we rose and headed toward her room to start packing her things. She would be back, I knew that, but my gut still turned at the thought of her not being around.

Twenty-One

AFTER HENTIE HAD LEFT, I DRESSED BARKINGTON in another of his knit sweaters, gave him a doggy treat, and promised him that he would see Hentie again soon. The goodbye had been tearful, and poor Bark had howled plenty. I'd done my best to console him with promises that she would be back soon enough or that we'd drive down to see her if we had to, but it was awful.

"Come on, Bark," I said, as I strapped him into his crate. "You and I are going to be the best of friends. Let's go out and have some fun together."

And by fun, I meant going to see Penelope and Ben at their home.

Barkington gave me a feeble wag of his slim tail, which didn't make me feel any better. I missed Hentie already, and it had barely been a couple of hours.

I hadn't even gotten the chance to tell her about my discoveries, and I doubted she would have wanted to hear about them when she had bigger issues to deal with. Family came first.

My heart ached at the thought.

Twenty minutes later, I parked outside Penelope and Ben's single story home. A brick building, with a sliver of a front porch. The path hadn't been cleared away properly, and there was a thin layer of ice covering it.

"This way, Bark." I held him against my chest, and we traversed the snow together, then carefully took the stairs until we reached the front door. "Safe."

He yapped agreement. I pet his head then knocked on the door.

It drifted open under my gloved fist. "That's not good," I murmured to Bark.

He whined.

"—think I'll stay with a man who cheated on me, you're out of your mind!" Penelope yelled inside the house.

The cold wind blew past me and down the hall, which had portraits of Penelope and Ben together, holding hands, and even a few of their wedding day. They had been happy, large smiles, cake smeared on their faces, and first dances.

"Please," Ben said. "You've got to believe me. I was

never going to leave you. Never. It was just a moment of weakness."

"A moment of weakness?" Penelope asked. "How many moments of weakness in a row does it take until it stops being a moment and just starts being weak in general? That's what you are, Ben. Weak. Pitiful. A wretched nothing of a man."

I covered Barkington's ears with my gloved hand.

"How can you talk to me like that? After everything we've been through?"

"You mean, after everything you've put us through? I'm leaving you, Ben. You can expect to hear from my lawyers within the week." And then Penelope burst into the hall from an open doorway near the end of it. She rolled a suitcase behind her and didn't even stop when she saw me standing in front of the open door.

I moved aside as Penelope wheeled her case onto the porch. She took a hard left and went down the side steps that led toward the garage. She nearly slipped and caught herself. "And you didn't de-ice the darn path!" She screeched.

I didn't blame her. It was a health hazard. And Ben was a cheat.

Ben stormed into the hall, opening his mouth to yell, but spotted me standing there. "What do you want?" he snapped. "Why are you here? Can't you see we're in the middle of something."

A door slammed and a car engine started.

Penelope squealed out of the driveway and took off down the street.

Ben glared after her, his arms folded and his blond brows drawn inward. They were so blond it looked as if he didn't have eyebrows, which was disconcerting.

"Sorry to interrupt," I said. "But I'm friends with Celeste, and I thought you ought to know she's in jail."

"I already know that. It's all over town, as is the news that Celeste and I were seeing each other."

"She said you were in love." I stepped into his house without invitation, but didn't close the door.

"We were involved, not *in love*."

"And you're okay with her being in jail?" I asked. "For a crime she didn't commit?"

"No, I'm not okay with it," Ben replied, irritably. "But what am I supposed to do? My life is falling apart because of this. I—" His expression hardened. "That darn Sheriff Stalz. If he hadn't been so set on solving the case of the Halloween Killer, none of this would have happened."

I didn't comment. It was better to let people talk. Sometimes, I was even surprised how much information you could get by shutting your mouth. People loved to fill the gaps in conversations. It made them feel less awkward.

"He's such a... I don't want to use curse words, but he deserves them. He's always been like this. Thinks he knows better than everyone else. Even in school. I'll never forget how he used to get people in trouble."

"He did?"

"Oh yeah," Ben raged. "He got me in trouble with the principal because I cheated on a math paper. And you should've seen what he did to the librarian."

My heart skipped a beat, but I kept my expression intrigued but not alarmed.

"He got him fired," Ben said. "Apparently, Mr. Stone was less than friendly to Harry Stalz, and nobody was mean to Harry Stalz. He told his homeroom teacher that Mr. Stone had physically accosted him. It was enough to get him fired."

"But surely, there must have been proof."

"Oh, he came to class with a black eye, but all of us knew he'd given it to himself. For heaven's sake, his girl-friend at the time told us after the fact that she'd caught him blackening his eye." Ben rolled his eyes. "Not that Belinda was any better. She was a piece of work too. Very unpopular. Picked on the other kids, and— What?"

"Belinda O'Toole?"

"Yeah, did you know— Hey? Hey! Where are you going?"

I marched out of the door and leaped off the porch

into the snow, landing with Barkington carefully tucked in my arms. I reached the truck and strapped him into his crate.

"I know who it is, Bark," I said. "I just have to prove it."

"Where are you going?" Ben called. "I wasn't done talking yet."

I had the connection.

The blurry picture on my corkboard had cleared.

An image of the night of the Halloween party, of Sheriff Stalz glaring, a look of utter disdain on his face, his upper lip lifting on one side. His gaze was fixed on Juniper, who was in the middle of torturing Celeste with her words.

And then the other images flashed in front of my mind.

An article lauding Sheriff Stalz as a hero for saving those girls from drowning. The articles that showed all the victims had one thing in common. They had been either mean, unpopular, or a threat to the peace in Cakeville.

My profile. A male, average height, mens size 13 shoes, who had kept trinkets. Trinkets that were trophies of his victories. Because he considered himself a vigilante. A man who made a mockery of those who had wronged him.

His dedication to "catching" the killer and cleaning up the town.

Sheriff Stalz thought he had pulled off the perfect crimes.

But that was only because he had no idea who he was dealing with. Me.

And Barkington too.

Twenty-Two

I PUT BARKINGTON IN MY ROOM WITH HIS WATER, pee pad, and a bowl of food, then gave him a kiss on the head and promised to return soon. Then I headed back out again, grabbing my utility belt on the way.

Brian passed me in the hallway and gave me a small smile but quickly averted his gaze. I did too. He wouldn't stop me. Our kiss had made things so awkward between us that it worked in my favor. He hadn't noticed the fanny pack in my hand.

I got into the I Scream for Ice Cream truck and locked all the doors then gripped the steering wheel in my gloved hands and took a breath.

Sheriff Stalz had already made his arrest. He had made himself the hero of the town. There was zero chance he would get arrested for the killings without hard evidence, and even then, I couldn't be the one to deliver the evidence.

If I knocked him out, tied him up, and disappeared from the scene, after placing the evidence beside him, the deputies would be suspicious and it would make the news. But we'd settled in Cakeville, and it would be suspicious if we took off again.

But Hentie's back in Texas. We could drive to her hometown.

Brian would be furious with me. He would never forgive me for pulling something like this again, especially after I'd done a similar thing just over a month ago.

But what choice did I have?

I gnawed on my bottom lip, going over the pictures again in my mind.

There had to be a way to expose the sheriff without blowing my cover at the same time, or drawing the public eye to the truck.

It's warmer in Texas. Still cold, but certainly warmer than Wisconsin. People would buy ice cream *and* hot beverages. We could make fried ice cream. I'd hoped to sell Berry Ripple ice cream this week, but we'd barely gotten the chance, and though Edna had bought a few tubs for her freezer, it didn't help us.

Do it.

I drove to the sheriff's house. After the arrest, Edna

had bragged about how the sheriff lived in an opulent shiplap home befitting of his status and had given me the street name when I'd asked. Like he was some celebrity on a star-studded tour map.

The house was pretty, with ice blue walls, a tiled roof that was covered in a fine layer of snow, and a wraparound porch, but the garage doors were closed. And the curtains were drawn. Nobody home? Sheriff Stalz was surely down at the department celebrating his "victory" in arresting Celeste.

Don't hate me for this, Brian.

I got out of the car, pulling on a beanie and tucking my hair underneath it, and made my way up to the front of the house. The door had a cutesy inlaid colored glass window. I used my gloved fist to punch through the glass, reach inside, and let myself into the house.

I entered, heedless of the crunching of glass underfoot. My focus was evidence. I searched thoroughly—a study, the kitchen, the living room, even the bathrooms, the bedrooms, until finally I found a loose board in the guestroom underneath the bed.

Let's hope it's something.

I lifted the edges of the board, then removed a worn journal from underneath the floorboards. Hurriedly, I opened it and laid it flat.

Most of the journal was empty, but scribbled in the

middle pages was a set of coordinates, along with a few entries written in a shaking hand.

> I've done it again, and I'm not upset about it. She had it coming. The way she talked to people in this town, the way she made them feel, it was worth it. I'd kill her all over again if I could. She looked perfect with that witch hat on her head. Goodbye, Juniper.

I had him.

I turned the page and read the next entry.

> I don't know why, but when things start getting... aggressive, I black out. I think it's because I see it as a job, getting rid of these people who bring the town down. I think it's because I wouldn't be able to handle it otherwise. I don't regret killing them. I don't regret humiliating them by making them part of those displays. I want the town to be clean. I want them to live in fear.

I paged forward.

Juniper will be the last one. Now that I'm sheriff, I'm going to have to play by the rules. Arrest the troublemakers instead. Celeste is next on my list. Having affairs with married men? I can forgive Ben, he was trapped by her feminine wiles. I think I'll arrest her. I can get the judge to give me a warrant for her if I plant the right evidence in her trash.

So, not only was he a psychopath, but he was sexist too. A double whammy. Fun.

Quickly, I searched the coordinates on my phone, and my stomach whooped. They pinpointed the cave behind the Cakeville Chateau in the Cakeville Nature Preserve.

I returned the board back to its place under the bed in the guest bedroom then walked through the house. I placed the book on the floor, right in the middle of the hall, a few feet past the entrance to Stalz' living room with its fireplace and mantelpiece, bearing a crystal carafe of bourbon.

Finally, I shut the front door and locked it, then positioned myself behind the wall in the living room and removed a silver mallet from my fanny pack. I lifted my phone and scrolled through my contacts, with difficulty thanks to my gloves, until I found the sheriff's number. I'd saved it after he'd given me his card at the beginning of the week.

I hit dial and held the phone to my ear.

"This is Sheriff Stalz," he answered.

A shiver ran down my spine. I was used to encountering bad guys, but after seeing the body and what I'd read in the journal... It was chilling.

"Sheriff, is that you?"

"Yeah. Who is this?"

"It's April from the Cakeville Chateau?" I made my voice sound breathy. "I was just going for a walk when I passed by your house and, I don't mean to alarm you, but it looks like someone vandalized it."

"What do you mean?" Stalz' sounded positively scandalized. After all, who would vandalize the home of the incomparable Sheriff Harry Stalz, the hero of Cakeville?

"I don't know, I just saw what looked like a hole in your front window? Of your door? Like somebody had thrown a rock through it. I thought you should know. Just want to be a good citizen."

"Thanks, April. I appreciate that more than you realize."

Oh, I'm pretty sure I know exactly how much you appre-

ciate it. "I hope you catch whoever did it. Bye, Sheriff Stalz! Congratulations on catching the Halloween Killer." Laying it on thick, but I got the vibe he'd like that—from the crazed ramblings and all.

"Thanks, April. Thanks a lot. Means so much." And he sounded ready to explode with pride.

I hung up, put my phone on silent, and tucked it away. And then, I waited.

Fifteen minutes later, a car pulled up in front of the house. I didn't move a muscle, but practiced slow, steady breathing, listening and waiting.

The door opened, and footsteps crunched over glass then stopped. "What—?" Stalz' voice, deep, shocked.

He'd seen the book.

As expected, he made a beeline for it. The minute he bent to pick it up, and his fingers brushed the cover, I stepped into the hall and thwacked the side of his neck with the mallet. He went down easy, and I didn't catch his fall. If he woke up with a concussion, well so be it.

I took zip ties from my fanny pack and secured his ankles and wrists, then walked to the door. I left it open, checked the coast was clear, and strode off into the fading dark, pulling my phone out to report a domestic disturbance at the address as I did.

Twenty-Three

Two days later...

"YOU WOULDN'T HAVE ANYTHING TO DO WITH this, would you?" Brian slapped down a copy of *The Cakeville Chatter* on the coffee table between the armchairs in front of the fire.

I didn't immediately look up from feeding Barkington a treat. We'd had a rough morning, mainly because Hentie had called, and we'd both gotten a bit emotional, Bark and me.

"April?"

"I've been meaning to talk to you," I said. "Barkington and I miss Hentie a lot. We think it would be a good idea to take a drive down to Texas and go visit her. It would certainly be warmer for the winter. Don't you think that's a good idea?"

"April, look at the newspaper, please." I looked up at his face, the serious expression, the downward curve of the corners of his lips. We still hadn't discussed that kiss, and I doubted we would for a while, but we couldn't avoid each other forever.

And I couldn't avoid his disapproval.

I lowered my gaze to the newspaper.

SHOCK AND HORROR: HALLOWEEN KILLER WAS LOCAL SHERIFF ALL ALONG!

Local sheriff, Harry Stalz, was arrested Tuesday after police arrived at the scene of an alleged domestic disturbance. On the scene, they reportedly found evidence linking Stalz to multiple deaths in Cakeville—all of the Halloween Killer's victims. Strangely, Stalz had been detained, but local law enforcement theorize that a burglar may have invaded Stalz' home, only to flee when police arrived.

Others have since come forward with more evidence implicating the Halloween Killer. Local baker and spelunking enthusiast, Wrenly Holmes, claims to have found several items related to the killings in a cave. The Casey County Sheriff's Department shut down the Cakeville Nature Preserve on Tuesday, shortly after making the arrest.

That was good. They thought it was a common robbery.

But it was time to leave.

"What do you want me to say? I'm glad they caught the guy," I said.

"Don't lie to me, April. We both know what's going on."

"Maybe you do," I said. "But I don't. And I'm not sure what you're insinuating."

"You want to play it like that, huh?" Brian asked. "After what happened, I thought maybe we—"

"Don't," I said. "Don't do that. Nothing happened between us. That's clear to me. Neither of us talked about it afterward, we're both awkward, we don't know each other, and we're forced to spend time together."

"What are you saying?"

"That we both know it was a moment of weakness," I said. "And it won't happen again."

"It wasn't for me."

"Do you really want to talk about it now?" I asked. "After you accused me of..." I tapped the paper. "Either way, I want to leave town and take the trip down to Texas."

"I haven't gotten word from Grandpa that we can do that."

I inhaled through my nose sharply. "I can't say that I care. Our friend needs us."

Smulder lowered his voice. "Your duty."

The words felt like a burden at this point. "Is to my friends, as well."

Brian stared at me, and I stared right back. "If you want us to move on, I can pass it on," he said. "I think you'll get approval because of what's been going on in town. But you're going to have to avoid making similar mistakes as you have in the past." He tapped the paper again.

"I hear you," I said, though I didn't like it.

Having that corkboard cleared off again was refreshing, but in a weird way, I missed the thrill of the hunt. Solving murders wasn't something I'd ever thought I'd do, or be interested in.

"All right. I'll touch base with you later on in the day," Brian said, and walked off.

Barkington yapped goodbye, and I hugged him tight.

"Oliver," I called.

Brian turned back and looked at me.

"Thank you. For asking," I said. "And it wasn't nothing. It's just—"

"Not right now?" he asked.

"Not right now." But maybe someday.

He gave me a smile, as if he could read the unspoken words on my face, then walked off.

I ate a cream puff and sighed as Edna entered the room

wearing another of her polka dot scarves tied around her head. She swept her arms wide to the room in greeting. "Good morning," she sang. "It's time for another fabulous day in Cakeville, my dears."

But it wouldn't be the same without Hentie, and we were going to remedy that. I pet Barkington's soft ears, my mind on the future, and when we'd meet up with our friend again.

Will Special Agent in Charge Grant let Delta and Brian leave to meet up with Hentie in Texas? Can Delta and Barkington solve another mysterious murder case? Find out in ALMOND SPRINKLE MURDER.

Craving More Cozy Mystery?

If you had fun with Delta Mission, you'll, love getting to know Charlie Mission and her butt-kicking grandmother, Georgina. You can read the first chapter of Charlie's story, *The Case of the Waffling Warrants,* below!

"Come in, Big G, come in." I spoke under my breath so that the flesh-colored microphone seated against my throat picked up my voice. "What is your status?"

My grandmother, Georgina—pet name Gamma, code name Big G—was out on a special operation. Reconnaissance at the newest guesthouse in our town, Gossip. The reason? First, she was an ex-spy, as was I, and second, the woman who'd opened the guesthouse was her mortal enemy and in direct competition with my grandmother's establishment, the Gossip Inn.

Who was this enemy, this bringer of potential financial doom?

A middle-aged woman with a penchant for wearing pashminas and annoying anyone who looked her way.

Jessie Belle-Blue.

It was rumored that even thinking the woman's name summoned a murder of crows.

"I repeat, Big G, what is your status?"

"I'm en route to the nest," my grandmother replied in my earpiece.

I let out a relieved sigh and exited my bedroom, heading downstairs to help with the breakfast service.

In the nine months since I had retired as a spy, life in Gossip had been normal. In the Gossip sense of the term. I'd expected that my job as a server, maid, and assistant would bring the usual level of "cat herding" inherent when working at the inn. Whether that involved tracking down runaway cats, literally, or providing a guest with a moist towelette after a fainting spell—tempers ran high in Gossip.

What was the reason for the craziness? Shoot, it had to be something in the water.

I took the main stairs two at a time and found my friend, the inn's chef, paging through her recipe book in the lime green kitchen. Lauren Harris wore her red hair in a French braid today, apron stretched over her pregnant belly.

"Morning," I said, "how are you today?"

"Madder than a fat cat on a diet." She slapped her recipe book closed and turned to me.

Uh oh. Looks like it's time for more cat herding.

"What's wrong?"

"My supplier is out of flour and sugar. Can you believe that?" Lauren huffed, smoothing her hands over her belly while the clock on the wall ticked away. Breakfast was in two hours and Lauren loved baking cupcakes as part of the meal.

"Do you have enough supplies to make cupcakes for this morning?"

"Yes. But just for today," Lauren replied. "The guests are going to love my new waffle cupcakes, and they'll be sore they can't get anymore after this batch is done. Why, I should go down there and wring Billy's neck for doing this to me. He knows I take an order of sugar and flour every week, and I get it at just above cost too. What's Georgina going to say?"

"Don't stress, Lauren," I said. "We'll figure it out."

"Right." She brightened a little. "I nearly forgot you're the one who "fixes" things around here." Lauren winked at me.

She was the only person in the entire town who knew that my grandmother and I had once been spies for the NSIB—the National Security Investigative Bureau. But the news that I had helped solve several murders had spread through town, and now, anybody and everybody with a problem would call me up asking for help. A lot of them offered me money. And I was selective about who I chose to help.

"I'll check it out for you if you'd like," I said. "The flour issue."

"Nah, that's OK. I'm sure Billy will get more stock this week. I'll lean on him until he squeals."

"Sounds like you've been picking up tips from Georgina."

Lauren giggled then returned to her super-secret recipe book—no one but she was allowed to touch it.

"What's on the menu this morning?" I asked.

Lauren was the boss in the kitchen—she told me what to do, and I followed her instructions precisely. If I did anything else, like trying to read the recipe for instance, the food would end up burned, missing ingredients or worse.

The only place I wasn't a "fixer" was in the Gossip Inn's kitchen.

"Bacon and eggs over easy, biscuits and gravy, waffle cupcakes and... oh, I can't make fresh baked bread, can I?"

"Tell her I'll bring some back with me from the

bakery." Gamma's voice startled me. Goodness, I'd forgotten about the earpiece—she could hear everything happening in the kitchen.

"I'll text Georgina and ask her to bring bread from the bakery."

"You're a lifesaver, Charlotte."

We set to work on the breakfast—it was 7:00 a.m. and we needed everything done within two hours—and fell into our easy rhythm of baking and cooking.

My grandmother entered the kitchen at around 8:30 a.m., dressed in a neat silk blouse and a pair of slacks rather than the black outfit she'd left in for her spy mission. Tall, willowy, and with neatly styled gray hair, Gamma had always reminded me of Helen Mirren playing the Queen.

"Good morning, ladies," she said, in her prim, British accent. "I bring bread and tidings."

"What did you find out?" I asked.

"No evidence of the supposed ghost tours," Gamma said.

We'd started hosting ghost tours at the inn recently, so of course Jessie Belle-Blue wanted to do the same. She was all about under-cutting us, but, thankfully, the Gossip Inn had a legacy and over 1,000 positive reviews on Trip-Advisor.

Breakfast time arrived, and the guests filled the quaint dining area with its glossy tables, creaking wooden floors, and egg yolk yellow walls. Chatter and laughter leaked through the swinging kitchen doors with their porthole windows.

"That's my cue," I said, dusting off my apron, and heading out into the dining room.

I picked up a pot of coffee from the sideboard where we kept the drinks station and started my rounds.

Most of the guests had gathered around a center table in the dining room, and bursts of laughter came from the group, accompanied by the occasional shout.

I elbowed my way past a couple of guests—nobody could accuse me of having great people skills—apologizing along the way until I reached the table. The last time something like this had happened, a murder had followed shortly afterward.

Not this time. No way.

"—the last thing she'd ever hear!" The woman seated at the table, drawing the attention, was vaguely familiar. She wore her dark hair in luscious curls, and tossed it as she spoke, looking down her upturned nose at the people around the table.

"What happened then, Mandy?" Another woman asked, her hands clasped together in front of her stomach.

Mandy? Wait a second, isn't this Mandy Gilmore?

Gamma had mentioned her once before—Mandy was

a massive gossip in town. Why wasn't she staying at her house?

"What happened? Well, she ran off with her tail between her legs, of course. She'll soon learn not to cross me. Heaven knows, I always repay my debts."

"What, like a Lannister from *Game of Thrones*?" That had come from a taller woman with ginger curls.

"Shut up, Opal," Mandy replied. "You have no idea what we're talking about, and even if you did, you wouldn't have the intelligence to comprehend it."

The crowd let out various 'oofs' in response to that. The woman next to me clapped her hand over her mouth.

"You're all talk, Gilmore." Opal lifted a hand and yammered it at the other woman. "You act like you're a threat, but we know the truth around here."

"The truth?" Mandy leaned in, pressing her hands flat onto the tabletop, the crystal vase in the center rattling. "And what's that, Opal, darling? I'd love to hear it."

"That you're a failure. You sold your house, left Gossip with your head in the clouds, told everyone you were going to become a successful businesswoman, and now you're back. Back to scrape together the pieces of the life you have left."

"Witch!" Mandy scraped her chair back.

"All right, all right," I said, setting down the coffee pot

on the table. "That's enough, ladies. Everyone head back to their tables before things get out of hand."

Both Opal and Mandy stared daggers at me.

I flashed them both smiles. "We wouldn't want to ruin breakfast, would we? Lauren's prepared waffle cupcakes."

That distracted them. "Waffle cupcakes?" Opal's brow wrinkled. "How's that going to work?"

"Let's talk about it at your table." I grabbed my coffee pot and walked her away from Mandy. The crowd slowly dispersed, people muttering regret at having missed out on a show. The Gossip Inn was popular for its constant conflict.

If the rumors didn't start here then they weren't worth repeating. That was the mantra, anyway.

I seated Opal at her table, and she pursed her lips at me. "You shouldn't have interrupted. That woman needs a piece of my mind."

"We prefer peace of mind at the inn." I put up another of my best smiles.

Compared to what I'd been through in the past— hiding out from my rogue spy ex-husband and eventually helping put him behind bars when he found me—dealing with the guests was a cakewalk.

"What brings you to Gossip, Opal?" I asked.

"I live here," she replied, waspishly. "I'm staying here while they're fumigating my house. Roaches."

"Ah." I struggled not to grimace. Thankfully, my cell phone buzzed in the front pocket of my apron and distracted me. "Coffee?"

"I don't take caffeine." And she said it like I'd offered her an illegal substance too.

"Call me if you need anything." I hurried off before she could make good on that promise, bringing my phone out of my pocket.

I left the coffee pot on the sideboard, moving into the Gossip Inn's spacious foyer, the chandelier overhead off, but catching light in glimmers. The tables lining the hall were filled with trinkets from the days when the inn had been a museum—an eclectic collection of bits and bobs.

"This is Charlotte Smith," I answered the call—I would never get to use my true last name, Mission, again, but it was safer this way.

"Hello, Charlotte." A soft, rasping voice. "I've been trying to get through to you. I'm desperate."

"Who is this?"

"My name is Tina Rogers, and I need your help."

"My help."

"Yes," she said. "I understand that you have a certain set of skills. That you fix people's problems?"

"I do. But it depends on the problem and the price." I didn't have a set fee for helping people, but if it drew me away from the inn for long, I had to charge. I was technically a consultant now. Sort of like a P.I. without the fedora and coffee-stained shirt.

"My mother will handle your fee," Tina said. "I've asked her to text you about it, but I... I don't have long to talk. They're going to pull me off the phone soon."

"Who?"

"The police," she replied. "I'm calling you from the holding cell at the Gossip Police Station. I've been arrested on false charges, and I need you to help me prove my innocence."

"Miss Rogers, it's probably a better idea to invest in a lawyer." But I was tempted. It had been a long time since I'd felt useful.

"No! I'm not going to a lawyer. I'm going to make these idiots pay for ever having arrested me."

I took a breath. "OK. Before I accept your... case, I'll need to know what happened. You'll need to tell me everything." I glanced through the open doorway that led into the dining room. No one looked unhappy about the lack of service yet.

"I can't tell you everything now. I don't have much time."

"So give me the *CliffsNotes*."

"I was arrested for breaking into and vandalizing Josie Carlson's bakery, The Little Cake Shop. Apparently, they found my glove there—it was specially embroidered, you see—but it's not mine because—" The line went dead.

"Hello? Miss Rogers?" I pulled the cellphone away from my ear and frowned at the screen. "Darn."

My interest was piqued. A mystery case about a break-in that involved the local bakery? Which just so happened to be run by one of my least favorite people in Gossip?

And when I'd just started getting bored with the push and pull of everyday life at the inn?

Count me in.

Want to read more? You can grab **the first book** in *the Gossip Cozy Mystery series* on all major retailers.

Happy reading, friend!

Made in the USA
Las Vegas, NV
16 September 2024